CRESCENT CALLING

THE CRESCENT WITCH CHRONICLES - BOOK ONE

NICOLE R. TAYLOR

CHAPTER 1

S tanding in the shadow of the ancient hawthorn tree, my grip tightened around the dagger.

I wished I'd opened my eyes sooner because it would've saved a lot of heartache, but it was always the way. Hindsight was a terrible thing in the aftermath of life-altering events. The past can't be changed, no matter how hard you wish it to be.

Sometimes, a coincidence is just that. Other times, the signs just keep piling up one after the other until there's no denying it. This was real. All of it.

Magic, witches, fae, shapeshifters. They no longer resided on the pages of a storybook. They lived in my backyard, clawing at my door, thirsting for the magic that ran through my veins.

Staring up at the hawthorn tree, the silver rays of the full moon trickled through the branches, dusting the clearing with an eerie glow. Under different circumstances, it might've been beautiful, but I wasn't waiting for a lover to come and sweep me off my feet. I was waiting for a monster.

The ritual was complete, the trap was set, and now all

that was left to do was to wait for destiny to come and claim me.

The sound of something moving through the woods echoed all around, and I spun, my heart leaping into my throat. Catching sight of the russet-colored fur of a fox melting through the forest, I sighed in relief. It was just him.

He stepped into the clearing and came to join me in the shadow of the hawthorn, a comforting companion in the dark of night.

"Do you think they'd be proud?" I asked my friend. "Are you sure we're doing the right thing?"

The fox yipped softly.

"My first test as the last Crescent Witch," I murmured, holding the dagger flush against my chest. "No turning back now."

It was my duty to protect the last whisper of magic from the darkness that threatened to take it. It didn't matter what I wanted. Not anymore. I was the only thing standing in the way of its extinction. Me. Skye Williams.

But my story didn't start here. It began on the beaches of southern Australia, an entire world away from the forests of Ireland, and the day I found out my mother had died.

The day the Crescents called me home.

The ocean was calm today.

Usually, the wind chopped up the water and hurled it at the cliffs down the coast, making it treacherous for the cargo ships leaving the bay. Passing between the headlands required the help of specialized pilots who zoomed out in their bright orange speedboat at all hours of the day and night, but today, the water was flat, and the wind hardly blew at all.

The sky was clear, though storm clouds brewed on the horizon, and the whole world seemed balanced on a knife's edge. Something was in the air, and it tickled up and down my spine like I was full of static electricity. The next time I touched something metal, I was going to get one hell of a shock.

It was the first of April, and there I was sitting on the deck of my dead father's beach house on the wild and windy coast of southern Victoria, Australia, like the April fool I was. Last night had culminated with a horrid confession from my boyfriend, Alex, rather than the passionate kiss I'd been expecting when the clock ticked over at midnight. Things had been great between us, and there I was thinking he was going to offer me a diamond ring. Fat chance.

He'd said it. *It.* The thing every woman dreads when she's expecting the complete opposite. The five words that resembled the ultimate cop-out when breaking up with someone. *It's not you, it's me.*

My grip tightened around the glass of 'water' in my hands, and the ice clinked. *Bastard.*

Pair that with being handed a redundancy package from my job the month before and I was onto a winner. Pulling my feet up onto the deck chair, I curled in on myself. Bad things always went for the trifecta. What was number three going to be? It felt like the universe was aligning for the ultimate slap in the face, and it was aimed right at me.

If Dad were here, he would know what to do. He always knew the right thing to say. *Buck up, kiddo. He just wasn't as good as your old man. There are plenty of other fish in the sea.*

Dad was gone now—he passed away from brain cancer, four months after his diagnosis—but his house was still here. He'd left it to me in his will, and I'd been too attached to it to even think about selling up. Good thing for me since I was broke and alone. I needed a place to crash until I could work out what I was going to do. So, I'd legged it from that awful party, passed Alex's place to pack my things, and had driven from Melbourne straight to Ocean Grove. I'd driven home.

The sound of screeching tires echoed through the stillness, and the glint of sun hitting metal glistened between the scraggly windswept scrub. A silver car appeared over the rise and weaved along the unkempt driveway toward my little beach house. I watched as it finally stopped, coming to rest next to my little red sedan in the yard, and the handbrake made a ratcheting sound as it was pulled on.

A balding man was inside, and I could see he was wearing a suit and tie. He flung open the door and wrestled with the seatbelt, and once he'd unclipped it, he practically fell out of the driver's seat and onto the patchy grass underneath. Then he dived back in, his stubby legs flapping about before finally emerging with a black briefcase. The whole thing was like a slapstick comedy routine out of a Monty Python movie, and I watched in silent awe at the display.

Narrowing my eyes, I wondered if he had the right house. He was wearing a dark suit, his tie done up, and his jacket still on. Lawyer? Debt collector? The odds were at two to one. His forehead was dripping with sweat as he waddled up the path, cursing under his breath.

Standing, I set down my glass on the table and leaned against the railing of the deck. "Can I help you?"

"Ah," he said, glancing up at me. "Are you Skye Williams?"

"Yeah." I looked him over and tried to hold onto my laughter. He looked like a penguin waddling up the path, and his short stature didn't help one bit, nor did his thick Irish accent. He was a long way from Antarctica.

"My name is Robert O'Keeffe," he said, dabbing his forehead with a handkerchief. "I'm here on behalf of you mother, Aileen."

I stared at him, my amusement turning into full-blown shock. I hadn't heard from her since I was two years old, and even then, I couldn't recall a single thing about the woman. All I had were a few creased photos and the random memories Dad used to mumble before he died. The meds the doctors put him on loosened his tongue, and for the first time in my life, I'd learned a little about the ghost of my mother, the Irish woman who'd come to Australia for adventure and ended up with my dad.

"My mum?" I asked the man. "You mean the woman who abandoned my dad and me when I was two? What does she want?"

The man, Robert O'Keeffe, wrung his hands. "I'm very sorry to be bringin' the news, but your mother has passed on."

I raised my eyebrows.

"It happened a month ago," he went on, looking forlorn. "I'm very sorry for your loss."

I raised my eyebrows. I was supposed to feel something, wasn't I? Sadness, shock, despair, or whatever emotion was comparable, but I didn't feel anything. How could I when I didn't even know her? My mother was a stranger.

"How?" I asked instead. Looked like morbid curiosity was now a thing with me.

"Heart attack. It was very sudden."

I snorted and glanced out across the ocean.

"I know this is a shock to you," he said, climbing the stairs and standing on the deck next to me. "But she left you everythin' she owned. I'm a longtime friend, but I'm also the executor of her will."

Everything was numb. Even the strange weather wasn't bothering me anymore.

"I guess that means I'm stuck with her debts now," I drawled. Glancing up at the sky, I added, "Thanks, universe. Just what I need. Just add bankruptcy to the pile, and you've got your trifecta. I knew something was coming today. *I knew it.*"

"No, no," Robert said, watching me curiously. "She had no debts. You can be sure of that."

"Then give me some good news, Robbie," I said with a scowl. "I lost my job to a cheaper workforce overseas, my boyfriend dumped me last night, and now you show up in your suit and tie and say my stranger of a mother has died. I'm a financially ruined, emotionally whiplashed orphan. Give me your best shot."

He beamed at me. "Aye, you're the spittin' image of her with your long black hair and green eyes, to be sure. She was just as strong willed with the mouth to match."

Another tidbit of information had just fallen into my lap, and I wasn't sure how to take it. When I was little, I'd always dreamed of her. I would lie in bed—cuddling whatever soft toy was my favorite that week—and dream up wild stories of what she would be like. She was from a faraway place that seemed so magical to a little girl of seven. Ireland with its green hills, wild forests, and fairies. Adventure...it seemed its call was in my blood.

Robert set his briefcase down on the table and popped the latches open. When he lifted the lid, he pulled out a pile of papers and a pen that glinted gold in the clear autumn sunshine, never mind the fact we were standing in the shade. The thing looked solid. As in twenty-four karat.

"I need some signatures to make it official, but here's the list of her assets." He cleared his throat and began to read. "*To my daughter, Skye, I leave all my earthly possessions and assets. The cottage I have called home for twenty-five years, which has been in our family for a hundred and fifty more, that resides in the village of Derrydun, Ireland. My shop, Irish Moon. All my belongings and inventory. The bank accounts and whatever remains in them.*" Robert shuffled another paper and read the amount, "Thirty-five thousand euros in the savings account. Twenty-eight thousand euros in the business account. Forty-six thousand euros in the term deposit."

"Whatever," I said, trying to keep calm about the one hundred and eleven thousand euros, not to mention the house and that Moon thing. It was about time she gave me something other than heartbreak. "Where do I sign?"

"I must warn you," he said, holding out the pen. "There's one condition that needs to be upheld."

I snatched my hand back. "Which is?"

"As her last living relative, you must come to Derrydun. Your mother stipulated it in her will," he said. "All costs associated with your travel will be looked after by her estate, but the condition still stands. You must come to Derrydun to settle."

"I have to go to Ireland?" I exclaimed. "But that's on the other side of the world!"

He nodded. "To be sure. That's how geography works."

"Oh, man..." I let my head fall into my hands before glancing up again. "Wait... I'm the last living relative?"

"Yes."

"What happened to everyone else?"

Robert frowned. "They passed goin' on twenty-five years now."

Putting two and two together, I began to form a picture of my mother's circumstance. She'd returned to Ireland and had never come back, but I didn't realize it might have to do with something like that. Everyone else had died, and she'd gone back. Great, this was going to be one of those deep, dark family secret scenarios, wasn't it? Did they have cults in Ireland?

Ignoring the lawyer—I presumed that was what he was —I studied the colors in the ocean. Deep blue, turquoise, greens, and dark blobs of black seaweed floating about in the current, at the mercy of the tides. Then there was the whole thing about the tides being at the mercy of the moon, and...well, it just went on and on. Everybody was controlled by something bigger than themselves. Employment, finances, global stock markets. I was unemployed, broke, dumped, and was moving into my dad's beach house in the middle of nowhere. There were great job prospects in a town of two hundred people. *Not.*

What did I have to lose by going to Ireland? Not a lot. Maybe I could finally understand why she, *Aileen,* left us behind and get my inheritance along the way. That money would come in real handy.

"Okay," I declared. "Give it to me."

Reaching out, I grasped the pen and yelped as a bolt of static electricity cracked through my fingers and up my arm.

"Curious," Robert declared. "That hasn't happened before."

"Holy..." I shook my arm, still grasping the pen. "That hurt like hell!"

"You know what they say about a static shock? It awakens things inside you that were sleepin'."

"No one says that. Do they?" I asked, rubbing my arm.

"No, I just made it up." He laughed and pushed the papers toward me. "Sign everywhere there's a sticky note. There's nothin' predatory in there, by the way. It's only for the name of ownership, which will be finalized when I see you in Derrydun."

I gave him a look before flipping open the contract and signing. The pen scratched over the paper, the ink as blue as the sea before us. Flipping over the last page, I signed and gave him back his solid gold pen.

"Here." He handed me a plastic folder printed with the details of a local travel agent. "Your ticket is already booked. You just have to call the agent, and give them your details."

"Were you that sure I would agree?" I asked, taken aback.

"When people are presented with free money, they usually say yes," he said with a deadpan voice. "It's life. Sometimes, you need a break, and that's what parents are for."

I made a face. "Fair enough."

"It was nice to meet you, Miss Skye," he said. "I will see you in Derrydun."

"Wait, you're not traveling with me?"

"No, I can't. But you'll do just fine." He closed his briefcase with a bang and clipped it shut. "Things always have a curious way of workin' out for the women in your family. Of that, I'm sure." Smiling mysteriously, he held out his hand.

I didn't know what else to do, so I shook his proffered hand.

"One last thing," he said, hesitating on the edge of the deck. "Your mother loved you a great deal, Skye. I was told your name was on her lips when she...you know."

I didn't reply. When it became apparent I wasn't going to offer him anything in response, he turned and waddled down the path, squeezed into his car, and drove away just as erratically as he'd driven in.

Glancing down at the folder from the travel agent, I sighed. I was going to Ireland. Checking the date on the ticket, I yelped. I was going to Ireland *the day after tomorrow*.

It wasn't until I went inside and called the travel agent in town that I realized the strange lawyer known as Robert O'Keeffe had no way of knowing I would be at the beach house.

Curious was the word of the day.

CHAPTER 2

Green rolling hills passed by in a flash as I drove across the Irish countryside.

I'd landed at Dublin International Airport at the ass crack of dawn, bleary-eyed after a twenty-six-hour flight from hell. A quick stopover in the middle hadn't helped much, but I was finally in Ireland and on my way to Derrydun, which the map told me was in County Sligo.

A rental car had been pre-booked, and to my joy, I'd been driving across an unfamiliar country with its funny road signs and imperial measuring system for the last three hours. Miles or whatever. Half were in kilometers due to some random change in the law and no one seemed to know how far away anything was for sure. Things seemed really close but were actually really far away. Thus, the three-hour drive I was currently enduring.

Following the directions the GPS gave, I took the turn off the main highway and traveled down a smaller road through some fields and then a forest before buildings began to shimmer through the trees.

Ahead, I spied a sign that read Derrydun *(Doire Dún)*. I

assumed the last bit was the village's name in the Irish language. All the signs had been like it on the way here. Attempting to pronounce the words, my tongue knotted up, and I sighed.

The road twisted and turned, but the village hadn't come into sight yet. Was it that small I'd already driven past? I glanced at the GPS, beginning to think I'd gone too far or had missed a turnoff. Rounding a bend, a tree loomed directly in front of me, and my heart skipped several dozen beats.

"Holy shit!"

I swerved, and the rental car careened around the tree, across the street, and sailed into a coach bay beside a quaint little cottage with a thatched roof. I came to an abrupt halt, my whole body sliding forward and back as I planted my foot on the brake.

My hands tightened around the steering wheel, and I took a few deep breaths while my heart returned to a healthy rhythm. A range of curse words revolved through my mind, and I reached down and flipped the key in the ignition, turning the beast off before I accidentally put my foot on the accelerator and drove into the creek in front of me.

Getting out of the car, I slammed the door shut and breathed in the clear country air. Welcome to Derrydun, indeed. At least the sun was shining, and I wasn't freezing in my dress.

Glancing around the little village, the first thing I noticed was the lack of noise. There was zero traffic, zero pedestrians, and zero human noise. I wasn't used to it.

Really, the whole place looked like it was out of a children's picture book. There were cottages with thatched roofs that had been turned into shops selling arts and crafts, a few whitewashed buildings bordered the road, there was a traditional looking pub covered in some sort of red leafed creeper, and overlooking the scene were ruins of some kind on the hill.

Where there wasn't a building, there were masses of green. Trees, flowers, babbling brooks—the works. It was so quaint I almost threw up.

Farther up the street was a single set of traffic lights and a modern service station. I had no idea what they needed the lights for since the road was deserted. I was the only fool on it.

When my heart had stopped trying to claw its way out of my chest, I spotted Robert across the street where he was talking to a much taller man. They'd obviously witnessed my near miss with the tree, and my cheeks flushed. What an entrance.

Robert raised his hand in a wave and waddled over. I glanced at the man he'd been standing with, but he'd already walked off.

"What's that tree doing in the middle of the road?" I exclaimed with a huff. "I nearly took it out!"

"It's a hawthorn," the lawyer said with a chuckle. "We build around because it's bad luck to cut them down. They're the trees of the fairies, you know. They're supposedly the mystical doorways into the fae realm."

I raised my eyebrows. "If you say so. They should put a sign or something." I waved my hand at it.

"Was your trip enjoyable?" he asked.

"Until the tree incident, it was as fun as being stuck in a tin can for twenty-six hours straight."

He smiled, not put off by my irritableness at all. "Welcome to Ireland. It's good to have you home."

Home? I wasn't so sure about that. This was my mother's

home, whoever she'd been, and I had no connection to this place whatsoever. I was a stranger in strange lands. Hell, I couldn't even understand the accent half the time, and we were all speaking the same language.

"Here are the keys," Robert said, handing over a heavy padded envelope. "I know you've traveled a long way, so I'll come by afore the funeral with the final paperwork."

"You're just handing me the keys without a signature?" I asked, peering into the envelope. "Just like that?"

"You're Aileen's daughter."

"So that's a thing? Like a discount card?" I made a face.

He shrugged. "You'll find Irish Moon right there." He pointed to a shop across the street. "And Aileen's cottage is directly behind it. The two-story bluestone with the garden."

"Irish Moon?" I asked with a frown.

"Your mother's shop."

I followed his pointing finger, but instead of finding the shop, my gaze collided with the strangest scene. There was an old man shuffling down the road, leading a donkey with a scrappy little Jack Russell terrier perched on its back.

My mouth fell open as they approached. It was a mirage. I was tired as hell from the flight and the death-defying drive over from Dublin, and now I was hallucinating.

"All right, Fergus?" Robert asked as they passed.

"Right," the old man muttered.

"That's a thing?" I asked, watching the procession with wide eyes.

"To be sure," the lawyer said. "Fergus is a local institution. He sells his handwoven crosses of St. Brigid to tourists right there. Has for years. You should get him to make you one. Brigid of Kildare is one of the patron saints of

Ireland. Besides, old Fergus would like you more if you did. Bein' Aileen's daughter isn't a discount card."

I snorted and rolled my eyes. "Thanks, Robert."

"Anytime. The funeral is tomorrow at the church. I'll come and get you in the mornin'."

I nodded. "Tomorrow, then."

The lawyer waved and waddled down the street, his ill-fitting suit hindering more than it helped his image.

Irish Moon sat across the street. I looked both ways before I crossed, but there hadn't been any traffic the whole time I'd been standing there. A wrought iron fixture was screwed into the facade, and a pale purple sign hung from the black metal. The lettering was done by hand with a crescent moon painted behind.

A girl was sitting on the footpath by the door, dressed from head to toe in black with big combat boots on her feet. Her eyes were dark with matching eyeliner, and her long, dyed black hair hung in her face. As I approached, the hiss of loud music coming from her earphones floated through the air. The whole ensemble reminded me of myself as a teenager. Rebellious to the point Dad pulled out his hair, hardcore into punk music, leather jackets, blue hair, and underage partying.

She was fiddling with her phone, and when my shadow fell over her, she glanced up.

"About time," she said, pulling the earbuds out of her ears and rolling her eyes. "I've only been waitin' here for an hour."

"Excuse me," I said haughtily. "I didn't realize there was a timetable."

The girl pushed to her feet and pointed to the sign hanging inside the door. "Openin's at ten."

"I just got here!" I exclaimed throwing my hands into the air. "And how do you know I'm not a customer, huh?"

She looked at me and shrugged. "You look just like Aileen."

"And who are you?"

"I'm Mairead," she declared like it was already a known fact.

"And what's a Mairead?"

"Mairead's a shop assistant," the girl said.

"Shoot." I opened the envelope Robert had given me and fished around for the keys. Pulling out two sets, I offered them to her. "I had no idea my mum had a shop. Do you know which key it is?"

Mairead plucked a set out of my hand and unlocked the door. "Are you tired?" she asked as we walked into the dark store. "People say you come from Australia?"

"People say?" I asked, beginning to feel nervous.

"Yeah." She turned on the lights, illuminating the cornucopia of crystals and gems. "It's all anyone's talkin' about."

"I don't know if I'm worthy," I muttered, distracted by all the shiny stones. I held the envelope against my chest and moved through the shop, studying every nook and cranny. Mum used to sell all this stuff? It was kinda...cool.

"What are you goin' to do with the shop?" Mairead looked at me expectantly.

"I really don't know. I didn't know my mum owned a shop until this morning. I think Robert mentioned it, but it was a shock, you know."

"Well, I can teach you how everythin' runs," she said. "I've been workin' here after school and durin' the holidays for three years now."

I glanced around at the display cases of crystals, jewelry,

knickknacks, and books. The air felt strange here, like it was warm even though there was a chill to it. Running my fingertips over the slice of amethyst in front of me, I shrugged. What was the harm in it?

"I suppose it won't hurt to keep it running until I decide what to do."

Mairead grinned. It was such a shock considering her mopey Goth attitude I made a face.

"How old are you?"

"I'm eighteen," she said proudly. "Well, I will be eighteen in August. I finished school last year, and I've deferred University for a semester. I'm startin' at Trinity in Dublin after the summer. I was kinda countin' on this job for some extra money... I want to get me own place."

Movement caught my attention outside, and I peered through the shop window. I watched as a tall man began clipping the hedge bordering the car park opposite to where my rental sat. An old lady with silver hair done up in a wild-looking bun was leaning on a broomstick watching him work.

The man looked young, maybe in his late twenties or early thirties. He was a messy kind of handsome with his curly hair that had been cut short on the back and sides but left long on the top, so it fell into his eyes. His jaw was dark with stubble, and when he reached higher, his red flannel shirt rode up revealing a mighty fine rear end. *Damn.*

"That's Boone," Mairead said standing next to me. She seemed to have gotten over her excitement about the shop and was now intent on relaying the village gossip. "He used to stay with Aileen."

"He used to stay with my mum?" I raised my eyebrows and glanced at the man again. "Who is he?"

She shrugged. "He just turned up one day. Aileen said

he was the son of some old friend. Now he lives about a mile down the main road."

"What does he do exactly?" I watched as the old lady spied some kids picking some flowers poking through the hedge, lifted her broom, and started chasing them down the street. Boone dropped his clippers and began running after her, waving his hands frantically. If I weren't so irritated and jet lagged, I might've laughed.

"A lot of things," Mairead said, snickering at the scene outside. "He helps Mrs. Boyle—that's the lady with the broom—with her garden, he works in the kitchen at Molly McCreedy's, he does deliveries for Mary's Teahouse, and he works on Roy's farm."

I snorted, wondering how he found enough hours in the day to do all of those jobs. Down the street, he'd caught the lady known as Mrs. Boyle and was coaxing her back toward her house. His arm was over her shoulders, and he was talking earnestly in her ear. Finally, he pried the broom out of her gnarled grasp and held it out of reach. Mairead didn't seem concerned with the scene, so I assumed it was a regular occurrence.

"He's really nice," she added. "He's the only one who can get Mrs. Boyle to calm down."

"Does she do that a lot? Chase kids like that?"

She laughed and nodded. "Beware of her broom. One day, it'll be an urban legend."

Turning my attention back to Boone, I studied his shock of curly brown-black hair, his stubbled jaw, and his broad shoulders and decided he was handsome. It wasn't a stretch to imagine what was underneath those trousers with the way they clung to his ass and all. I tilted my head to the side and made an appreciative face. *Nice.*

As if he'd read my mind, he glanced up, his gaze zeroing

in on the shop window where Mairead and I were blatantly staring at him. The girl raised her hand and waved, but my cheeks flared red, and I turned away.

"So how does this place work?" I asked, smoothing down my dress awkwardly.

"Aren't you tired?"

"I'm trying to stay awake until it's normal bedtime." I shrugged.

"Well, the whole village is shuttin' down tomorrow for Aileen's funeral," she said. "But I can help as much as you want today."

"Is there much business?" I asked, wondering if everything closing was the Irish version of a state funeral. "It seems really quiet."

"Oh, yeah," Mairead said excitedly. "Tons of tourist buses stop all the time. Mostly from now until October, but there's always someone comin'. It's quiet now, but just wait."

Looking out the window where Boone was still cutting Mrs. Boyle's hedge, I grimaced. It was quiet now...but the whole village would be on top of me tomorrow with their questions and stories. What was I supposed to say to them?

"Well, we'd better get started with my training," I said to Mairead. "Today, you're the boss."

The cottage behind Irish Moon was a two-story bluestone building that looked just like the rest of the village. The garden was in full bloom with purples, yellows, oranges, and reds all over the place. A vegetable patch was at the side where another door was set into the wall, and in front of me was the main entrance.

I was afraid to go in, so I stood there, the keys heavy in

my hand, my suitcase at my feet. I'd moved the silver rental car into the space behind the house once the tourist coaches started arriving, and just like Mairead had said, business was booming.

Derrydun had already surprised me in more ways than one.

Sighing, I grasped the handle of my suitcase and rolled it up the path. The only thing I knew about my mother was she'd left us—a man who loved her and a helpless toddler. She'd left us all alone. I was the spitting image of her, which mustn't have been easy for Dad, and now here I was about to step into her home. Twenty-five years of my mother sat behind that door. What if she turned out to be a real bitch? Or worse, what if she was *nice*?

Unlocking the door, I opened it and was immediately hit with the scent of home. Somehow, it was familiar, and as I stepped over the threshold, everything tingled with static like it had the other day at the beach house. Shivering, I closed the door and found the light switch in the hall, then flipped it on.

To my right was a sitting room filled with furniture with unfashionable floral coverings, an open fireplace, and a television in the corner. A bookshelf sat against one wall, overflowing with all kinds of tomes. Straight ahead was a staircase, and to my left was the kitchen. Naturally, I went for the food first.

Leaving my suitcase in the hall, I stood by the table. Everything here smelled earthy. Wet and woody with a hint of rosemary and mint from the herbs by the back door.

There was a note on the table from Robert detailing how the heating worked and that I would find some welcoming gifts in the fridge. The lawyer had thought of everything, and I was grateful. Now that I was here in my mother's home, it really hit me. I would never get a chance to know her. Not really. She was gone, and I hated that it had taken her death to finally bring me here. Needless to say, I wasn't going upstairs. Not tonight.

Opening the fridge, I found a bunch of casseroles inside with notes taped to them. Flipping over the first one, it was from some people named Fiona and Mark Ashlyn. Friends of Mum, I suppose. At least I wouldn't have to worry about finding something to eat for a while.

Taking out the top container, I set it on the bench while I opened and closed all the cupboards and drawers looking for a plate and some cutlery. Dishing out a healthy portion of some lamb concoction, I watched it rotate in the microwave. Aileen cooked her meals here. The evidence she was a virtuoso in the kitchen was all around. Battered pots and pans hung from the wall, herbs were drying in bunches in the window, and tired-looking recipe books were propped up on the counter.

The microwave beeped, and I pulled out the steaming dish. Sitting at the table, I stared into space, wondering how in the hell I'd gotten from there to here.

She was all around me but still so far away.

CHAPTER 3

I stared at the gravestone in front of me and sighed. The Celtic cross reached up into the blue sky, the stone worn from enduring hundreds of years out in the harsh Irish elements.

Here lyeth the body of Mary Byrne, who departed this life on the... The rest was unreadable.

"Ah, you found your ancestor," Robert said, appearing beside me.

He'd turned up at the cottage that morning as promised, I'd signed the last of the paperwork with his posh gold pen, and it was done. Everything my mother had owned now belonged to me. I was expecting some kind of closure, like a book snapping shut, the moment I signed the last bit of paper, but nothing happened. Nothing at all. It was such an anti-climax.

"She was related to me?" I glanced at the lawyer and back to the headstone again. We had different family names.

"Aye. This one's an old one. Died seventeen somethin'." He rubbed his hands together and bounced from foot to foot. "It's chilly out here. Do you want to go inside?"

"I thought it was almost summer?"

"Summer? What's summer?" He laughed and offered me his arm.

Watching the stream of people walking into the church, I made a face. Mairead was right. Everyone had turned up for the funeral and had dressed in their finest black outfits to boot. There were no corners for me to hide in once I walked through those doors. All eyes would be on me, the mysterious daughter of their beloved Aileen.

"Do I have to go in there?" I asked.

"I don't know what's worse. Goin' to a funeral or being stared at by the entire village. But strength in numbers, or so they say." He wiggled his arm like a chicken flapping its wings.

"Has anyone ever told you that you look like Danny DeVito?"

"You're a master, Skye, but I'm not fallin' for it. Let's go."

"But surely someone's told you," I said, taking his arm.

"Aye. I auditioned as his stunt double for that Batman film."

"Really?" The lawyer was earning some serious cool points.

"No," he said, bellowing with laughter.

"That's mean!"

"Now here's the church, so it's time to be serious," he said.

The sound of organ music filtered out of the open door, and I glanced around nervously. I caught a few pairs of eyes but quickly turned my attention to the grass underfoot. Sad smiles, curious stares, hushed whispers. I didn't like it at all. I didn't fit in. I was a stranger, and it felt a great deal like them versus me.

"Skye, this is Father O'Donegal," Robert said, dropping my arm. "He runs things here at St. Brigid's."

Turning my attention to the priest, I smiled politely. He was an older man with white hair, wrinkled skin, and watery eyes. His collar was done up tight, the little white bit at the front signaling his priestliness.

"It's lovely to meet you, child," he said taking my hand in both of his. "I'm sorry it has to be on such a sad occasion, but welcome to Derrydun. My door is always open."

"Uh, thanks," I muttered.

"Come. We've saved you a seat at the front right by your mother."

I almost choked on my own spit as Father O'Donegal led me into the church, down the middle aisle, and directed me to sit front and center.

The fancy reddish brown coffin had been placed directly in front of the altar, and thankfully, it was closed tight. I suppose this was as close as Aileen and I were going to get on a physical scale.

"Goody," I muttered, sliding my ass onto the hard wooden pew.

"It's on this day, we've come together to farewell our beloved Aileen McKinney," Father O'Donegal began, his voice droning at the one note. I bet this was his church voice. "She never came to church or followed the Catholic faith, but she was still a pillar of our community and requested we all gather here today to celebrate her time on this earth and wish her a fond farewell on the path to the next life."

I slumped back against the pew and let my thoughts wander as he opened his Bible and began to read. The side door was open, letting in some fresh air and a ray of sunshine. I studied the light playing across the stone floor and noticed how it made the gold on the altar shine. I was never a church person. I'd never prayed, or gone to a service, or stepped inside one out of curiosity, so I didn't know what any of it meant.

Glancing at the coffin, I suppressed a shudder. Aileen had died a month ago, and she was in there. What did she look like now? Not right now—that would be gross. What did she look like before she'd died? I only had pictures of her when she was young. Narrowing my eyes at the coffin, I shivered. The whole scene weirded me out.

I felt an unseen force burning into my back, and I covertly peered over my shoulder. A pair of dark eyes were staring right at me. *Boone*, aka the hot Irishman. When he noticed I'd caught him, he quickly turned his attention back to Father O'Donegal's sleep-inducing sermon.

Settling back into the pew, I held onto the sigh that was trying to work its way out of my lungs. He'd caught me checking out his ass, and now he was staring at me in the presence of my estranged mother's coffin. That wasn't awkward at all.

Movement outside drew my attention, and I narrowed my eyes as a tabby cat wandered inside. Nobody moved except me. I glanced at Robert, but he was listening to Father O'Donegal's sermon looking completely enraptured. The cat padded around the front of the coffin, disappeared for a moment, and then jumped up onto the altar.

I began to squirm, wondering why no one was shooing it away. The cat prowled across what I presumed was the sacred table of the Lord, sat at the far end, and began licking its front paw. I stared at it in subdued shock while Father O'Donegal continued reading from his bible like nothing was out of the ordinary. He didn't even skip a beat, and none of the villagers in the church batted an eye.

When it was done with both front paws, it cocked a leg and started licking its balls. It's big, tomcat balls.

I gasped, the sound echoing through the silent church. Everyone turned and stared at me, and I slapped my hand over my mouth. A cat was licking its balls center stage, and they were looking at me? *Seriously?*

Father O'Donegal snapped his Bible closed, and the cat leaped from the altar. Calling the pallbearers forward, the organ started playing again.

"There's no eulogy or anything?" I whispered to Robert.

"Your mam wasn't big on those kinds of things," he replied. "I think her words were 'Let the Father have his moment, and just drop me in the hole.'"

Scowling, I watched the six men she'd chosen come forward and pick up her coffin. The mysterious Boone was in front, and I couldn't help my dirty look from becoming filthy. Who was he to Aileen? Why was he so special when I was nothing?

I hung back as the procession moved outside and lingered on the fringes as her coffin was lowered into the ground, shaking my head and smiling politely when people offered to stand aside so I could be nearer. The whole day had felt like I was going through the motions, almost as if I were completing something on a checklist of things to do. Witness mother's funeral so I could claim my inheritance. *Check.* It wasn't right, but there wasn't anyone else.

When everyone started to disperse, chatting between one another, I backed away. I didn't get far before Robert, my constant shadow, spied me lingering awkwardly on my own.

"Skye," he said, forging a path through the crowd. "It was a nice service, don't you think?"

"There was a tabby cat sitting on the altar the whole time," I said with a scowl.

"Oh, that's Father O'Donegal's cat," he said, waving his hand. "Pay him no mind."

"Even when he licked his balls?"

"Welcome to Derrydun," the lawyer said with a chuckle. "It's a magical place."

"It's...eccentric." Old men with dogs riding on donkeys, ball-licking cats in church, Goth girls in crystal shops, hot guys with a thousand and one jobs, crazy broom-wielding grandmas...the list went on.

Robert chuckled. "All the best places are."

After that came the crushing wave of mourners. A blur of faces passed before me in a solo procession as Robert gave their names, and they gave their condolences, offering me stories about Aileen.

That man was Roy, whose farm bordered the village. That was the guy who owned the pub. That sweet little lady was Mary Donnelly from the teahouse. Those people were the Ashlyns who gave me that tasty casserole. Mairead and her parents swung by for a chat, telling me how excited they were that Irish Moon was staying open for the summer, which was news to me. Some other people made themselves known. More names were thrown in my face. More sweet stories about how lovely and caring Aileen had been and how much she'd given to Derrydun.

It hadn't even been a week since I found out she'd died, and paired with traveling from the other side of the planet to be here, I felt the beginnings of a panic attack tearing at my frail patience. I excused myself and legged it around the side of the church, finding myself among the dead once more. At least they couldn't talk. Dead men told no tales and all of that.

Leaning against a solid-looking headstone, I breathed in deeply. The air was so crisp here it hurt my lungs and made my head spin. There was something about this place that felt odd, and it had nothing to do with its eccentric population.

Footsteps crunching on gravel drew my gaze, and I found the hot Irishman walking toward me. His hands were shoved into his trouser pockets, and his tie was loose and skewed slightly to the side. I noticed he was wearing a pair of well-worn black boots, which were a stark contrast to all the shiny shoes the other men had donned. He wasn't used to wearing a suit—that much was clear.

He approached somewhat nervously, his gaze raking over me with unmasked interest.

"I'm Boone," he said, smiling lopsidedly. "You must be Skye."

"What gave it away?" I replied with a sigh.

"The accent for starters."

"I stick out like a sore thumb, huh?"

"I just wanted to offer me condolences... Aileen was like a mother to me."

I scowled. "Well, at least she was to somebody."

He stiffened and began to backpedal at an alarming rate. "I didn't mean to offend you..."

"I..." I clamped my mouth shut and roared in frustration. Spying a path beside the graveyard, I made a break for it, leaving the mysterious Boone in my dust.

I strode down the path, my feet crunching on gravel, desperate for some space. Soon, trees gave way to an open lush field dotted with black and white sheep, bordered by a haphazard stone fence. I dragged myself up the incline, the power in my legs starting to wane.

Ahead were the ruins I'd spotted on the hill the day before. It looked like some kind of tower, all crumbled and covered in moss and vines. A tree was growing on the inside, its trunk splitting the ancient wall until they had become one. I wondered who'd lived there.

Coming to an abrupt halt, I stared up at the ruins, a weird tingling rushing up and down my spine. It was...nice here. Better.

Thinking about everything that had happened at the church, my irritableness began to simmer down. I suppose the hard part was done now. The funeral was over, and Aileen was buried, so now I could take a breath and pull myself together.

What now?

"Skye!"

I turned at the sound of Boone's voice and cursed under my breath. He'd followed me down the path and up the hill, and his presence made my blood pressure rise again. And here I was thinking a hot guy running after me would excite all my naughty bits and be completely romantic. All I was thinking about was smacking him with my right hook instead.

"I'm sorry," he said, standing a few paces away. "I didn't mean to offend you."

"You didn't have to run after me," I muttered. "I'm a big girl."

He began wringing his hands together and glanced down at the village below. Silence opened up between us, the complete absence of noise freaking me out.

"I will never be able to understand what it was like for you, Skye. All I can tell you is what I know. Aileen loved you."

My hands began to shake as anger rose hot and hard at his words. If she loved me, then where was she? If she couldn't come home, then where were the letters, the birthday cards, and the phone calls? *Where was she?*

Glaring at Boone, I exploded. "Everyone down there is telling me what a wonderful woman she was, and all I can think about is how she abandoned me! I don't know her, and she didn't know me. She wasn't there on my birthdays. She wasn't there at Christmas or at stupid school plays. She especially wasn't there when my dad died of brain cancer! But I was. I was there for it all. What a wonderful woman! I'm sorry for *your* loss!"

A sob burst from deep within my chest, and before I could stop myself, tears practically exploded out of my eyes *Exorcist* style. Boone reacted immediately, pulling me into his arms.

"It's gonna be okay," he crooned in a soft, soothing voice. "You'll see."

I allowed him to comfort me for a moment before pulling away with embarrassment. He was a stranger—a hot stranger—and I'd left a wet patch on his white shirt.

"I don't know what I'm supposed to do," I mumbled, wiping at the stain. "You all expect me to be... I don't know. Like her, I suppose."

"For what it's worth, I expected you to be like you."

I couldn't meet his gaze. The hot Irishman I'd only just met, ranted at like a lunatic, and bawled in front of all in the space of half an hour. I was really put together.

"That's the thing about Derrydun," he added. "If you need help, all you need to do is ask. Doesn't matter who you are."

Staring past him, I focused on a baby tree growing just off the edge of the field. It shuddered and leaned toward me in the most unnatural way, and I gasped. My reaction seemed to set it off, and it snapped back into place.

"What's the matter?" he asked, stepping toward me. "Are you all right?"

"That tree," I said, wiping at my tears. "It…"

Boone glanced to where I was pointing and smiled.

"That's a hawthorn saplin'," he said, not noticing how it had moved all by itself. Kneeling beside it, he ran his fingers over the leaves. "This is a good omen if you believe in those kinds of things."

"How?"

"Hawthorns are full of magic. They guard the doorways into the realms of the fair folk among other things."

"Fairies?" I snorted. "They're just stories."

"Perhaps." He shrugged and rose to his feet. "This land is old and full of wild stories. A new hawthorn is still good luck."

I definitely needed some of that.

"Everyone's goin' to Molly McCreedy's," he said. "Will you come?"

"To who?" I asked with a frown.

"Molly McCreedy's is the pub." He waited, and when I didn't reply, he added, "There's good food, drink, nice people… I'll go with you."

"I… I don't think…"

Boone smiled lopsidedly and held out his hand. "Don't you want to see a bit of Irish craic?"

"Crack?" I asked, making a face.

"*Craic*. It means fun."

Looking at his hand, I shrugged, stepped around him, and began walking back down the hill. There would be alcohol at the pub. *Lots* of alcohol.

CHAPTER 4

If there was one thing I learned about the place my mother called home, it was that Molly McCreedy's was the heartbeat of Derrydun.

Stepping across the threshold, I glanced around with curious interest. I'd never seen anything like it.

The walls were full of framed photographs and paintings, the tables were all mismatched, the bar was made from a dark mahogany, and the golden beer taps glistened in the murky light. An open fireplace, covered with a wrought iron grate, was at one end, and over the mantle hung a painted portrait of a woman. The plaque set into the bottom of the gilded frame read 'Molly McCreedy — 1655–1687.'

Behind the bar were shelves packed full of bottles, most of them whiskey, and below were modern fridges full of craft beers and cans of larger. Beyond was a door that led through to the kitchen, which was in full swing given the assembled crowd.

The scent of wood smoke, stale beer, and cooking filled the entire place along with the riotous sound of a sing-along. Someone had brought a guitar and a tambourine, and it seemed cause for celebration. Whatever song it was, everyone knew the words and were shouting in unison, having the times of their lives.

Everyone clapped at the right moments during the chorus—four, two, then shouted hey!—and sung along with something close to reckless abandon. Nobody gave two hoots what they looked like. *This must be the craic Boone was telling me about.*

"Do you know this song, Skye?" a man I recognized from the funeral asked.

I shook my head.

"It's called *Whiskey in the Jar*," he explained. "It's about a man who steals some money from a ship's captain and is betrayed by a woman."

"Stop tryin' to talk her up, Sean," Boone declared behind me. "Give the girl a moment to catch her breath."

"I was only bein' friendly," the man named Sean grumbled.

The entire way here, Boone had followed me, keeping his distance. I wasn't sure what was more creepy—him following me up the hill in the first place or lurking behind me all the way down.

Ignoring the two men, I weaved through the packed room and found the bar. The moment I slid onto a free stool, a woman appeared before me. The first thing I noticed about her was her chestnut-colored ringlet curls and freckled nose. She would have to be around the same age I was, mid to late twenties. I wondered what she was doing here because the more people I met in this village, the more I realized the ratio of young to old in Derrydun swung a great deal more in one direction than the other.

"You must be the famous Skye," she said, leaning against the bar.

"Uh, that's me, but I'm not famous or anything."

"I didn't get a chance to offer me condolences today," she said. "I'm Maggie Ashlyn. Me da owns the next farm over from Roy's farm."

"Oh," I said, straightening up. "Someone told me about your dad. I think. Honestly, I can't keep up with all the names and places. Then there's the accent." I moaned dramatically.

"Tell me about it. Me da moved here from the UK when he married me mam. So I'm half and half, though I grew up here in County Sligo. People tell me my accent slips into one or the other from time to time. Just to confuse you." She winked. "Anyway, I'm sorry about your mam passin'. She was a lovely lady."

"So I hear." Jealousy was becoming my default setting the longer I was in Derrydun.

"Can I get you anythin' to eat or drink?"

"No, I don't really have much of an appetite."

Maggie smiled, then held up a finger. Turning, she selected a bottle from the shelf behind her and flipped a glass over in her hand. Pouring a few fingers of the brown liquid, she slapped the glass down in front of me. "Here, have a dram of whiskey. It'll warm you right up."

Knowing I was a complete lightweight, I sipped tentatively as the strong woody scent burned my nostrils. The alcohol went down my throat in much the same way as fire blazed along a line of gasoline. Coughing, I set the glass down and waved a hand at my watering eyes.

"Bloody hell," I cursed, then sipped again.

Maggie leaned against the bar with a smirk. "I see you came with Boone."

I glanced over my shoulder. He was standing with a group of men, laughing, his entire face lighting up. I was beginning to suspect he was the epitome of the Irish. Cheeky as hell.

"He followed me," I said. "I found my own way."

"I can see why he's interested in you," Maggie said. "He was very close with Aileen."

"So I hear." I straightened up. "Hey, what's his story, anyway? I was talking to Mairead at the shop, and she said he just turned up one day."

"That's about the gist of it." Maggie shrugged. "You can usually tell where someone is from due to their accent, and I hear a lot of them workin' behind this bar. Not just from the tourists who come through, either," she said. "At first, I thought he was from Galway. Then, the next day, his accent changed, and I thought he might be from Cork instead. Then he took on Sligo with a little bit of Dublin. So, no, I don't know where he's from. It seems our Boone is from everywhere."

Looking back over my shoulder again, I peered at him. The man from everywhere with his thousand and one jobs, his cheeky lit, and his roguish exterior. I hadn't felt this hot under the collar about a guy since...well, *ever*. I'd just looked at him and was all like *hello sailor*.

"Cute, ain't he?"

Jumping a mile, I grimaced. "I suppose."

Maggie laughed. "So what about you? What do you do back in Australia?"

My shoulders sank, and I rolled my eyes, but she was the first person to ask me about my life and not gush about Aileen and her impeccable standing in the community. It was just my life was in tatters right now.

"That good, eh?" she asked, raising an eyebrow.

"I *was* working for a big bank in Melbourne, but a month ago, they handed my entire department redundancies. Then they shipped our jobs to a cheaper workforce overseas. I'm an unemployed drain on society." I fist pumped the air with as much enthusiasm as I could manage. Which wasn't much at all. "I'm currently drifting."

"I'll never understand big business," Maggie said, shaking her head. "It's all cuttin' costs and budget this, bottom line that. That's why I like Derrydun so much. We look out for one another. It's about the folk right here, right now. I'm sorry to hear about your troubles."

"What about you? You've never wanted to go to the city?"

"Nah. I went to study in Dublin when I was nineteen, then to London for a year, but I ended up comin' home. There's just somethin' about this place..." She stared dreamily into the distance before squaring her shoulders. "Ah, that's another story for another time. I'm meant to be workin'. I'd better get back to it. Enjoy your night, Skye."

As she moved back down the bar to serve some locals, I swiveled around on the barstool. Nursing my whiskey, I surveyed the pub. People were laughing in groups, clinking glasses, eating hearty meals being ferried out by the kitchen staff, and the low strumming of guitar music could be heard over the din. If this was a wake, then it wasn't like any I'd seen before. There were no tears in sight.

Everyone knew each other and gravitated around the familiar in their lives, and here I was, the stranger. Taking another sip of my whiskey, I began to struggle with the odd sensation of being alone in a crowd. I couldn't even see Robert, and I wondered when the lawyer had left. Probably while I was up the hill with Boone.

At the thought of the hot Irishman, my gaze fell on him for the tenth time since I'd walked into the pub.

There was something about him I couldn't quite put my finger on, and it wasn't to do with his general hotness. Something else radiated around him almost like an aura. I'd always been a good judge of character to the point it had been like a sixth sense, but Boone...I couldn't figure him out.

Disregarding him, I turned my attention to the people standing around him, attempting to put faces to the names I'd learned that afternoon. Sean McKinnon, Mark Ashlyn, Roy, Mary, and Mairead's parents, Beth and Gregory. There were a ton more, but I'd already forgotten who they were.

Behind the group by the fireplace, a man was leaning against the wall, watching the room just like I was. Curious, I watched as the villagers milled around him but never once acknowledged his presence. Another loner like me.

Realizing he was being watched, the man raised his head and zeroed in on me. He stared back, his face shimmering as if he were some kind of freaky mirage. I blinked, and his skin darkened to a bluish gray, and his teeth elongated into sharp points before the whole image snapped back. Stiffening, I was frozen to the spot, unable to look away.

Something wasn't right. Wasn't this how psychosis started?

Boone appeared next to me, drawing my attention back to reality.

"Are you okay?" he asked, sitting beside me.

"I, uh... I'm just tired. I haven't had much time to rest." Looking across the pub, the strange man had disappeared.

Boone frowned. "Would you like me to walk you home?"

Craning my neck, I searched for the stranger but couldn't see him among the press of people.

"Lost somethin'?"

Shaking my head, I turned my attention back to Boone. "No, I... I'd better go home."

"Home, eh?" He grinned.

"It's a figure of speech," I retorted, springing off the stool.

"Maybe."

Rolling my eyes, I made a break for the door.

"Goodnight to you, Skye," he called out after me. "Be seen' you!"

It wasn't a long walk back to the cottage, but I couldn't shake the image of the weird man at Molly McCreedy's. If he'd been real at all.

Outside, the main street was lit, but behind Irish Moon, the garden was dark, and long shadowy fingers stretched across the vegetable patch. Shivering, I sank into my jacket and tried not to look back. The sensation of a hundred pairs of eyes watching my every move was freaking me out even though I knew I was alone. I suppose that was the problem. Anything could be lurking in the darkness where I couldn't see.

My boots crunched loudly on the gravel path as I hurried through the night. Fumbling for my keys, I stood under the eave and wrestled with the lock. The moment the door opened, a dark streak darted through my legs and disappeared into the house.

Letting out a yelp, my heart twisted, and I fell back against the doorjamb. *Was that a cat?* It had better be a bloody cat because I had no patience left to wrangle any wild beasts tonight. Were there any dangerous animals in Ireland? Did squirrels sneak into people's houses and attack their faces while they slept at night? Who knew. I *was* on foreign soil.

"Hey!" I exclaimed running inside and slamming the door closed behind me.

Bumping into the kitchen door, I turned on the light and spied a big tabby cat sitting on the table. It was watching me with its big green eyes, its tail flicking back and forth.

"Just make yourself at home, cat," I said with a pout.

It yawned, showing its teeth and bristly tongue.

"Well?"

It licked its whiskers and continued to stare at me.

"What do you want, hey?"

It blinked slowly and rose to its feet like it was going to pounce. Standing beside the table, I looked it over. It was quite a pretty thing. Large for a house cat, but its coat shimmered with a rich tabby color, and it even had a tinge of ginger.

"So, are you a boy or a girl?" Holding up its tail, I made a face. "Yep. You're a big boy all right. Are you Father O'Donegal's cat? If you are, then you made quite the scene at the funeral today." The cat headbutted me, nuzzling up for a pat. Placing my hand on his head, I scratched behind his ears. "You don't have a collar, though..." I glanced at the fridge. "Are you hungry? I've got chicken casserole."

The cat mewled and jumped off the table, making a run for the hall.

"Oh, no you don't!"

Chasing after it, I groaned as I saw it leap up the stairs.

"You had better come back down here!" I shouted, knowing full well cats were right little so-and-so's and never listened to anyone but themselves. It wasn't coming back down anytime soon.

Glancing up into the darkness of the second floor, I

grasped onto the balustrade. Who knew what lingered up there. Memories, smells, personal belongings, clothes, and knickknacks. All the things I didn't want to face.

I placed my foot on the first step, and it creaked. This was how horror movies began. *Get a grip, Skye.* Thundering up the stairs, I flung open the first door I found and saw it was a bathroom. The next door along revealed a bedroom—which, by the lived-in feeling, must've been Aileen's room.

Tiptoeing across the room, I found the lamp beside the bed and turned it on. The room was illuminated with a warm glow, revealing the cat had found his way to the most comfortable place in the house. Aileen's bed.

"Typical," I said, running my hand over his head. "Where have you led me, buddy?"

Turning my attention to the room, I began to add to the things I knew about my mother. A handmade quilt lay across the foot of the bed, the gold panels shimmering in the lamplight. The vibrant sun and moon design was kitsch and reminded me of a quilt cover I had as a child. I'd been obsessed with stars, and whenever Dad and I went to the beach house, we would sit out on the deck, and he would point out all the constellations he knew. Then I would spend hours staring at the moon, trying to make out all the craters through his battered pair of binoculars. Maybe Aileen had done the same thing before she left us, and this quilt was a reminder. It was a comforting thought.

Turning to the dresser, I ran my fingertips over a little tray of jewelry, studied a bottle of perfume, and peered inside a silver box. Opening the lid, my heart skipped a beat as I saw a familiar image. Picking up the photograph, my hands began to shake. The edges were worn, which meant it had been handled a lot. I knew because I had one exactly the same.

I stared at the candid snap of my dad, Aileen, and me and wasn't sure what to think. I was a baby in the image, barely old enough to open my eyes, but my parents were smiling at the camera with the beach I knew like the back of my own hand in the background. Boone seemed to think she loved me. He'd said as much that afternoon on the hill. Maybe the photo was proof she thought of us at least some of the time.

Sliding the photo back into the silver box, I turned. Staring at the bed, I sighed. Dare I? It would be better than another night on the couch. The cat began to purr happily and kneaded his claws on the bedspread.

"This is such a weird place," I said to the cat. "I'm either still jet lagged, or..." I shrugged. "I'm talking to a cat." I snorted and rubbed my eyes. "This is my mum's room, huh? Do you think she and Robert were, you know?" I snorted and shook my head. "No, I don't think so. Actually, I was beginning to think Robert's strangeness was just an Irish thing, but the more I get to know him, the more I think it's just because he *is* strange. Everyone here has their own quirk. What's mine? What was Aileen's? She had a crystal shop in an out-of-the-way Irish village. It's not exactly the same as the traditional handicraft store next door." The cat had opened his eyes and was watching me. "I mean, am I supposed to call her Mum, or what? It feels better to call her Aileen. For now at least."

Lying back on the bed, I stared at my new buddy, who'd closed his eyes.

"Do you believe in monsters?" I asked, stroking his back. "I think I saw one at the pub. A man with bluish-gray skin and pointy teeth." The cat meowed and curled up into a ball. "I know, right? I'm so tired I'm starting to hallucinate. It'll be better tomorrow. Are you going to hang out here tonight?" The cat didn't move, so I assumed he'd decided to stay over. "All right, but don't hog the bed, okay?"

The cat didn't even twitch.

Kicking off my boots, I shimmied out of my jeans and crawled underneath the covers. Burrowing into the sheets, I studied the stripes running through the mysterious cat's back before switching off the lamp.

There was no such thing as monsters. Hallucinations brought on by exhaustion, however...

CHAPTER 5

The next morning, the cat was gone.

After a frantic ten minutes searching for him, I couldn't find where he'd gotten out. All the windows and doors were locked tight. Scratching my head, I began to wonder if he was a mirage like the man at the pub had been.

When I opened the front door, double-checking for cat-sized escape routes, I saw a package shoved underneath the cheery welcome mat.

Bending over, I slid it out and saw my name written on the orange paper. Glancing around the garden, nothing stirred apart from the odd bird flitting across the lawn searching for fresh worms to feast on.

Taking the envelope inside, I turned it over, but there was no postmark or indicator as to who had left it. It had been hand delivered by someone, and I was positive it hadn't been there last night.

Sitting at the kitchen table, I tore the parcel open and tugged out a stack of papers. It was paperwork for Irish Moon. Robert must've left it.

Reading through the various reports and tax returns, I

was surprised at the figures. The takings were rather healthy for a little crystal shop in the middle of nowhere even if it was on the so-called tourist trail. Aileen had really built something here, but what was I supposed to do with it? Stepping into my mum's shoes and picking up her life as my own wasn't exactly something that had crossed my mind. It also sounded weird. I didn't want to be Aileen version two.

If I wanted to, I could sell up and go back to Australia. I wouldn't have to worry about getting a job straight away, not with the money that now sat in my savings account. Or I could travel for a while and see the world. With nothing and no one to hold me down, I could go anywhere.

The cottage and everything in it would fetch quite a bit considering its proximity to the village. Then there was Irish Moon and its inventory. What was I going to do with that?

"*Shoot!*"

Scraping the chair back, I grabbed my jacket, phone, and keys and ran from the cottage, slamming the door closed behind me. Hearing the latch lock into place, I legged it through the garden, leaped over the fence, and bolted to the street.

Mairead was leaning against the wall, waiting for me.

"I'm sorry, I'm sorry," I exclaimed breathlessly, fumbling with the keys.

The Goth girl looked rather cute today in a black dress, black boots, and her matching black hair done up in twin French plaits. When I appeared, she smiled brightly.

"It's okay," she said. "Sundays are quiet. Church is in the mornin', and the buses don't usually come until late if they come at all."

"Why aren't you at church?"

She made a face and gestured to her outfit. "Do I look like I subscribe?"

"Point taken."

Unlocking the door, I let us inside. Immediately, I was drawn to the little tubs of tumbled stones—amethyst, citrine, rose quartz, snowflake obsidian, and more—and dug my fingers into the colorful array while Mairead turned on all the lights and busied herself with opening the store.

I wasn't really into running a shop—at least, not right now—but she seemed to really enjoy it here. Maybe I should ask her if she would like to take on more responsibility. At least until I figured out where my heart lay. I thought about it for a moment, and it didn't seem like such a bad idea. She knew the ropes and said she needed the extra cash.

"What did Aileen pay you?" I asked.

"Nine euro an hour," Mairead replied, retrieving a feather duster from behind the counter.

"That doesn't sound like a lot," I said with a frown. "Is that minimum wage here?"

"You can pay me more if you want," the girl said with a grin. "I won't mind."

"*Right.*" I admired her tenacity. "Would you help me out this week, then? Full-time until I can work out what I'm going to do. That should help you out, right?" I did the math in my head. "Four hundred for the week? Then we can talk next Sunday."

Mairead's eyes lit up with dollar signs—or was it euro signs?—and she nodded enthusiastically. "I won't let you down, Skye."

I felt uncomfortable being in the power position, so I just shrugged. "You're helping my clueless ass out."

"If you want to take some time off, I can handle things here today," she added, swatting a large crystal with the feather duster.

Thankful for the chance at a break to gather my thoughts, I left Mairead to handle things at Irish Moon.

The sun was out today. Finding my way behind the row of shops, I followed a path that wound through a pretty copse of trees before opening up to a lush field and the tower on the hill. Dew glistened on the grass as I wandered, and the sound of water gurgling in the creek followed my footsteps. The air was cold for the turning of the seasons. Summer was only a handful of weeks away, but I was still layering on a jacket before I left the house.

Walking on autopilot, I wandered up the hill, following the path, my thoughts taking on the same rambling pattern. What was I going to do? How long was I going to stay? Did I actually want to know more about Aileen, or was it a perverse sense of duty that was forcing me to hesitate? Nevertheless, there was a deeper question I was avoiding in the shadow of the bad luck of the past month. What did I want to do with my life? The million-dollar question.

Realizing I'd reached the pinnacle of the hill, I glanced up at the ruins as I approached. A sign sat in front of the structure where the path opened up into a little cul-de-sac, bordered with some old railway sleepers that made the whole thing look neat and tidy. The ground was worn, which meant tourists from the buses that stopped in the village came up here to take a photo of yet another ruin that dotted the Irish landscape.

Stopping by the sign, I read the inscription, which had been embellished with an artist's representation of what the ruins would've looked like when it was intact.

The White Tower. 1635–1756.

The legend of Mary Byrne is one of the lesser-known tales of witchcraft from the period but nonetheless, one of the most intriguing. She lived in this very tower house, having married

Joseph Byrne, the Lord of Diore Dún. Their lands comprised of the village proper and several square miles of wild forest, which still stands today.

To the locals, Mary was known as a healer, using herbs and natural remedies to aid the sick and less fortunate. Though, through her kindness, she also found her end.

She was tried for witchcraft in 1756, found guilty, and burned at the stake. In the days after her death, the tower house was said to have mysteriously caught on fire. It may very well be true. Damage to the structure is consistent with high temperatures, and it leaves historians to wonder, was it purely a tragic accident? Or was it retribution from beyond the grave?

Snorting, I looked up at the ruins and attempted to pick out the marks the fire had left behind, but there was nothing there. Either I didn't know what I was looking for or time and weather had worn them away.

At some stage, someone had set a modern iron gate in the entrance to keep trespassers out of the site. Crossing the grass, the toes of my boots dampening with dew, I studied the exterior of the tower house. The crumbling facade was covered with yellow and gray lichens, and rich emerald moss clung between each slab. There was a wild and romantic feeling about this place that would look great on a postcard.

Curling my hands around the bars, I peered into the darkness that used to be someone's home. The earthen floor, the bare walls...I just couldn't picture it.

Nothing stirred. Not even the rustling of leaves overhead penetrated the bubble around the ruins. There was just... nothing. No sound and no movement, just the scent of wet earth and a strange tickling sensation on the back of my neck.

Shivering, I let go of the bars and retreated across the

grass, my feet arriving back onto the path. Suddenly, I felt really exposed and shrank into my jacket.

Hurrying back down the hill, the ruins at my back, I stopped for a moment to take in the view of Derrydun. From up here, I could almost see the whole village. There was Molly McCreedy's and Mrs. Boyle's house. The pink cottage with the thatched roof was Mary's Teahouse. To the left was the Topaz service station with its little convenience store. The one set of traffic lights was shining green on the side I could see, and while I was standing there, I watched as a car came hurtling up to the intersection with the red light, gave way for a moment, then peeled through. What was with the drivers here? They were just as mad as the inhabitants of Derrydun.

Despite the circumstances that brought me here, I was beginning to see the charm everyone talked about when they spoke of Ireland. The green rolling hills, the local flavor, the good food and drink, the stories, and the carefreeness of it all. Here, in this place, life seemed simple.

To my left, I spotted a red and black checked shirt lying over the stone fence. I found myself lingering when I recognized who it belonged to. Looking out over the field, I saw Boone forging his way through a flock of sheep, wearing a tight black T-shirt and loose-fitting jeans that were torn and dirty on the knees.

When he saw me, he raised his hand in a wave. I did the same, though more hesitantly.

Boone had been nice to me, regardless of his relationship with Aileen, which, by this stage, I was realizing was totally innocent. I doubt he was trying to go after my inheritance and undercut me. He didn't seem the type. Approaching the fence, I decided to drop my bristly exterior and give him a break.

"Is it always this cold in the mornings?" I asked, burying my hands deeper into my pockets.

He closed the space between us. "Aye, it can get chilly in these parts. Best you get used to it."

"I never thought I would miss the Australian summer," I replied.

"You feelin' better today?" he asked, leaning against the fence.

"Yeah. Thanks."

"You're not at Irish Moon today?"

I shook my head. "I gave the helm to Mairead."

His eyes crinkled at the corners. "That's brave of you."

"She needs the money for University or College or whatever you call it here." I waved him off. "She seems to know how it all works."

"Do you like the shop?"

"I'm...intrigued," I replied. "I never knew that about Aileen. That she was into all that new age crystal stuff."

"She spent most of her time in there, that's for sure."

"It feels warm in there. Better. If that's a thing." I shrugged. "People say crystals have all these energies. Maybe it's that."

"Perhaps." The conversation ebbed out for a moment before he nodded up the hill. "You've been up to see the tower house?"

"Yeah." Glancing over my shoulder, I studied the ruins until my eyes began to water. "It's such a sad story."

"The world wasn't always such a nice place for those who were different," Boone said, sounding rather philosophical.

"I suppose not."

We fell into an awkward silence again, and just like last time, he was the one who broke it.

"You're drawn to the older places," he said mysteriously. "The tower house, the hawthorn saplin', the crystals in the shop."

"I suppose," I said with a shrug.

"Don't you think it's curious?" he asked, wiping his brow with his forearm.

"No. Should it be?" I wasn't quite sure what he was getting at. Boone had this mysterious thing going on, but he was starting to speak in riddles. I wondered if it was an Irish thing or if it was his own personal quirk.

"Your mam was the same," he said. "She liked those places."

"Oh?"

We stood in silence for a moment, neither of us knowing what to say. I was never good at small talk, which was probably why I'd always had small friendship groups. All my friends had been Alex's first, so when we broke up the other day, I assumed I would never hear from them again. They knew him longer, so that's how it usually went.

"You and Aileen," I began.

Boone sprang to life. "Ah, I was homeless, you see, and she offered to help me get back on me feet."

"Really?" I tilted my head to the side.

"Aye, she offered me a room in her home, and Derrydun offered me as much work as I was able to accept."

"Okay."

"When she passed... I moved to a little place of me own a mile down from the village center," he went on. "It's a little rough around the edges, but it's comin' along. I like it."

Yeah, I reckon I was right taking back my earlier assumption of him. He seemed genuine, and I felt bad for giving him a taste of my trademark sass.

"It feels so long ago," I muttered, sitting on the fence.

"What does?"

"The day I found out... It was only last Monday. That means..." I sighed. No wonder my inner bitch was raging. "A month ago, I lost my job. Then my boyfriend dumped me last Sunday night, and Robert turned up on Monday telling me about Aileen. Two days after that, I was on a plane to the other side of the world, and then yesterday, Saturday, I buried the mother I never got to know. For the first time, I'm completely alone. That's my life in a nutshell." I glanced at Boone nervously. "I'm sorry, I've been mean to you this whole time."

"Don't mention it," he said with a lopsided grin. "I figured it would be a lot for you to take in. No offense taken."

"Nothing seems to faze you, does it?"

"There's always worry in life, that's how it works, but you can't let it stop you from bein' happy." He sat beside me and cast his gaze over the field. "Your boyfriend is a fool if you ask me. Lettin' a pretty thing like you go?" He shook his head. "*Cic maith sa tóin atá de dlíth air.*"

I narrowed my eyes, trying to ignore the part where he said I was pretty. "What does that mean?"

"It's Irish for he needs a good kick up the ass."

I laughed, slapping my hand over my mouth. "In Australia, we would say he needs a good kick up the clacker."

His smile widened, and he shoved his hand through his wild hair. It was a full-on modelesque pose, and my insides began to quiver. His T-shirt didn't leave much to the imagination, which didn't help, either. Realizing I was staring and developing a crush on the poor guy, I turned my attention to the sheep in the field. They were white with black faces and feet, and every single one had a line of brightly colored paint on their backsides. I wondered what it was for.

"Why are the sheep painted all different colors?" I asked.

"Ah, it's so everyone can tell which one is theirs," Boone replied. "They put them all into the same field, which is our way of sayin' we were too lazy to put up a fence."

I smiled, counting four different colors. There wasn't much artistic value in their markings, just a line of paint haphazardly slapped on each rump. Blue, red, green, and orange.

"Then there's Albert," Boone went on as a ram came into view. Well, I was fairly sure it was a ram since it had horns on its head. "He's a special sort around here."

I snorted as Albert's back end came into view. His backside had been painted in black and white stripes.

"*Sligeach*," Boone declared in Irish. "County Sligo Football Club."

"You painted a sheep's ass in football colors?" I asked, my mouth dropping open.

"Nay, I didn't," he said, trying to hold in his laughter. "Roy did."

I shook my head, knowing the more I was going to see of Derrydun, the stranger it would become.

"Do you like it here?" I asked, the question coming out of the blue.

Boone shrugged. "It's as good a place as any. People have accepted me here, I enjoy me work, and I suppose I've helped in me own way."

"Helped?"

"Small places like this, they thrive on community," he explained.

"I see." I stared down at the village, wondering what it

would feel like to be part of something bigger than myself. I'd floated for so long I wasn't sure what it would look like.

"Whatever you choose, Skye, you'll always be welcome here."

My gaze snapped up and met his, surprised at the accuracy of his declaration. It was like he could read my mind or my emotions or whatever. Either that or I was transparent as hell. My heart was stapled to my sleeve, or whatever the saying was.

"That seems rather farfetched," I said, making a face. "You've known me for five minutes. Are you sure you want to invite me into the clubhouse?"

Boone laughed, his roguish smile making my heart flutter.

"Of course," he said. "McKinney blood runs in your veins. You'll always be a part of Derrydun, no matter where you are."

As we sat there on the fence overlooking the village, I couldn't help the feeling of hope that tugged at my heartstrings. It would be nice to belong somewhere even if it was only for a moment.

CHAPTER 6

That night, the tabby cat came back, and by the time I'd woken the next morning, he'd disappeared again.

This went on for a few more days, and each time, I would search the house to find the spot where the little Houdini had wriggled out of but never found a crack big enough for a cat to shimmy through.

As for the cottage, I slept in the main bedroom, but I never ventured further, let alone opened the silver box on the nightstand again. I needed to make a choice, and knowing Aileen wouldn't make it any easier, so I decided not to know her at all. It would be easier that way.

I spent another few days in Derrydun, sitting in Irish Moon with Mairead and getting to know the lay of the land before I made my decision. The longer I stayed, the further away I floated from the life I knew. The familiar was blurring, and nothing felt like home anymore.

I thought about Boone and his scruffy handsomeness and Yodaesque philosophy on life. I thought about Mairead and Maggie, the two unlikely friends I'd made since being here. Then I thought about Robert O'Keeffe, the lawyer, and his dry sense of humor. He seemed to have disappeared after the funeral, and I wondered where he'd scurried off to. He probably had another orphan to deliver an inheritance to.

I thought about everything that had happened since I'd arrived, and it wasn't enough.

I woke up on the morning of my seventh day in Derrydun and decided I was going to sell.

When I arrived at Irish Moon, Mairead was waiting for me outside like she did every morning. Rattling the keys, I picked the right one and shoved it into the lock. Twisting, I heard the mechanism click, and I shoved inward, but the door didn't budge. Trying again, I swore under my breath. I didn't need this today.

"Stupid door," I cursed, kicking the doorjamb.

"That's never happened before," Mairead said, looking just as puzzled as I felt. "Let me try."

Taking the keys from me, she rattled them in the lock and pushed inward, but the door was stuck fast.

"Don't push too hard, or the glass will break," I said, watching over her.

"I know. I'm tryin'."

Elbowing her out of the way, I grabbed the door handle, turned the key, and shook. "Open," I commanded. "*I said open!*"

Abruptly, the door swung inward and crashed against the wall with a bang. Luckily, the glass didn't break, but Mairead and I stood there for a full minute with our mouths hanging open.

"Well, that solves that then," I declared, dusting my hands. Mairead just stood there, so I added, "C'mon. Get inside."

Mairead went in and started turning on all the lights on

her way to the storeroom at the back where she usually dumped her bag. The displays full of crystals began to shimmer and sparkle, and the stand of Irish themed wind chimes rattled musically as the outside breeze came in with us.

Closing the door, the bell rattled, and I rounded the front counter.

"I'm going to sell the business. Just so you know," I said, retrieving the laptop from the shelf under the till.

"No! You can't!" the girl exclaimed, emerging from behind the bookshelf.

"I'm sorry, but I have to." I thought about rattling off all the reasons I'd used to convince myself last night but shook my head. I didn't need to explain myself.

Mairead pouted and turned her back on me. Ignoring her, I fired up the laptop. I knew she was counting on the extra money, but I couldn't put my life on hold so I could do a girl, who I didn't really know, a solid.

Connecting to the shop's Wi-Fi, I opened a browser, typed in a search term into Google, and waited for the results to come up. The arrow turned into a colored wheel and started spinning as the laptop began to think a little too hard. There was a reason people had dubbed it the spinning wheel of death. Moving my finger over the trackpad and clicking, I knew the whole thing had frozen. *Seriously?*

Holding down the power button, I restarted the laptop and tried again, but the same thing happened. Kaput the moment I fired up a web browser.

"It keeps freezing!" I exclaimed, throwing my hands into the air. "How am I supposed to get anything done with this piece of rubbish?"

"It's a brand-new laptop. Aileen got it six months ago."

Mairead glanced over the display of tumbled stones and made a face. "So it's an omen."

"An omen for what?"

"That you should keep the shop," she said, rolling her eyes. "*Duh.*"

"I don't want to keep the shop," I declared. "This isn't the life I signed up for!"

"First, the door got stuck, and now your laptop won't work," the Goth girl went on, lifting a cardboard box from where it was hidden underneath the display. Opening the top, she began filling up the citrine, mixing the older stones with the new. "It's a sign."

"Don't signs come in threes?" I asked with a pout.

Mairead shrugged. "Who knows?"

Ignoring her, I turned my attention back to the laptop, which had restarted. Waiting for it to connect to the shop's Wi-Fi, I opened the browser and waited. And waited. Then the mouse pointer turned into the spinning wheel of death. *Again.*

"Fine," I spat, closing the lid of the laptop with a thud. "I'll fix you."

Taking out my mobile phone, I opened the web browser and searched for a local real estate agency. Finding a nice looking one in Sligo, I made the call while Mairead pouted sulkily at me.

I spoke with an enthusiastic Italian man named Fredrico something or other. Strange he was Italian and not Irish, but I supposed this part of the world was rather multicultural with the European Union and all of that. I'd never met someone from Italy before.

I explained the business, my circumstances, and he agreed to see what he could do.

"I have time," he said. "I'll stop by in an hour. Does that suit?"

"We're open all day, so that's perfect."

Once I'd hung up the call, Mairead pounced on me.

"Are we really that horrible?" she asked, glaring at me.

"What are you talking about?" I asked, scowling back just as hard.

"You've been here a week and already want to sell everythin'. You haven't given us a chance!"

I gasped dramatically and rose to my feet. "I didn't know this place existed!" I shouted. "My life is in Australia! Not here!"

"But—"

"But nothing," I said irritably. "I want to go home."

"You want to give up," Mairead muttered, turning her back on me.

"Excuse me?" My hackles rose.

"Aileen was nice to me," she cried. "She didn't care that I looked different. You don't even want to know your own mam!"

"She left me when I was two. What do you want me to do, Mairead?"

The girl was shaking with emotion, which put me on edge. "She might be dead, but you can still try."

My mouth fell open.

"You like it here, admit it," she said, practically stamping her foot. "You're pretendin' to hate it because you don't want to like anythin' to do with Aileen. I bet she had a good reason for comin' home. She always did, you know. She was wise and kind, and you're..."

"I'm what?" I asked, my face reddening in annoyance.

"Scared you might be just like her."

I didn't realize it until she'd thrown it in my face. Still, I just had to bite back at the poor girl to prove a stupid point. "And here I was thinking you were just chucking a tantrum because you would be losing your job."

Rounding the counter, I strode outside to wait for the real estate agent, leaving Mairead to pout to her heart's content.

Outside, Maggie was leaning against the wall, playing with her mobile phone. Standing beside her, I sighed.

"It's a little early for a bad day," the bartender said. "What's the matter?"

"Mairead is being a sulky teenager," I replied, thankful to see her. "I've decided to sell the shop, and she's up in arms."

"So you want to leave us?"

I groaned. "Not you, too."

Maggie shrugged and slipped her phone into her jacket pocket. "Nah, I just would've thought you would stay a little longer before you made up your mind."

"Them's the breaks."

"What are you doin' out here?"

"Waiting for the real estate agent. He's coming over from Sligo to evaluate the business."

"Ah, this will be him now, I suppose," she said as the sound of an approaching car hummed in the distance.

Behind us, the bell rang over the door as Mairead appeared. She glared at me and shook her hair defiantly. "Your boyfriend show up yet?"

"See what I mean?" I said to Maggie.

We lingered on the footpath, listening to the approaching car. When it appeared, zooming around the bend at an alarming speed, I realized the man behind the wheel hadn't seen the tree in the middle of the road. The look of horror on his face was priceless. If he weren't about to crash, I would've burst out into fits of laughter.

My heart skipped a beat as the car swerved around the hawthorn, careened through the coach bay, and splashed into the creek where it finally came to a halt.

Mairead began to laugh as the real estate agent kicked open the door—it was the one and only Fredrico because the name of the agency was on the side of the car—and tumbled out onto the ground.

"Oh, *cac*," Maggie said, her sides practically splitting open.

"What's *cac*?" I asked.

"It's Irish for shit," Mairead explained.

"I'll say," Maggie declared. "We're going to have to fetch Roy and his tractor now. It's going to cost the poor guy."

"The power of three," Mairead said. "I told you so!"

"What?"

"Three omens," she explained triumphantly. "First the door, then the computer, and now that guy's car crashin' into the creek."

"That's stupid," I declared. "There's no such thing as omens. You're just seeing what you want to see."

"Tell him that." She nodded toward Fredrico, who was ranting loudly in Italian.

Later, as I stood there watching Roy drag the car out of the creek with his tractor, and Fredrico told me he wouldn't sell the shop for all the commission in the world, I started to see things from Mairead's perspective. The power of three.

I wondered if fate was an actual thing or if Derrydun was some kind of vortex like the Bermuda Triangle. Strange things kept happening around me, and it wasn't anything to do with the villagers and their peculiar quirks. Something wanted me to stay. Desperately.

Once Fredrico had sped away and Roy was on his way back to his farm, I went into Irish Moon, feeling rather sheepish.

"You were right," I said to Mairead.

She leaned against the counter, cleaning up after the last busload of tourists had been through. Most of them had stood around watching the car being towed from the creek and taking photos, which didn't help my situation. Roy thought it was hilarious, so I was pretty sure the gossip would make its way around the entire village by the end of the day.

"What? I can't hear you," Mairead said, pretending to be deaf.

"I said *you were right!*" I screwed up my face and stamped my foot. "Okay? Don't rub it in. I don't want to know her because..." I sighed dramatically. "She left me behind with my dad—who's dead by the way—and you all worshiped her, okay?"

Mairead's triumphant smile faded, and she shrugged. "I suppose I'm sorry, too. I didn't think of it that way."

"Well, at any rate, it looks like I'm staying. For a while at least."

"It was really funny, you know." The girl smiled. "The car..."

I snorted and began to laugh. "It was, wasn't it?"

"I thought his head was going to explode."

"Imagine if his car hadn't started."

And just like that, Mairead and I became friends —*proper* friends—and Derrydun became a little more like home.

CHAPTER 7

The next day, I opened Irish Moon early.

If I was sticking around, then I had better start making an effort assimilating into village life. That meant taking an interest in the business that might end up being my job for the next fifty years. *Ugh, imagine that.*

Sitting behind the front counter, I began sorting through the papers that had been shoved underneath the till. Old receipts, delivery slips, and handwritten notes dating back years had accumulated in the little space, so I pulled them all out and put them into an old cardboard box from the storeroom. I would have to sort through them later.

Reaching back into the shelf to make sure I hadn't missed anything, my hand settled on a small box that had worked its way right to the back. It was a black rectangle with a metallic gold design etched into it. At first, I thought it might be a set of playing cards, but the box was a little larger than standard. Sitting on the stool behind the till, I shook my treasure, listening for a rattle. Something inside moved from side to side.

The box was covered in scuff marks, so I assumed it had

been opened and closed quite a bit before I stumbled on it. Easing off the lid, I found a stunning set of tarot cards inside. *Of course.*

They had to have belonged to Aileen. It was another thing to add to the list of things I knew about her. She read tarot. I wondered if she'd been any good and if she knew all the hidden meanings.

Tipping over the box, I emptied the cards out onto the counter. Picking up the first one my fingers found, I saw they were matte black with metallic gold designs, which shimmered as I tilted it back and forth. The deck was quite pretty to look at even though I didn't know the meanings. Scattering them over on the counter so I could see better, I studied the wands, swords, cups, and pentacles. There were also other cards like The Sun, The Moon, The Fool, The Emperor, and more. I knew they all had meanings and ones that deepened still when set with other cards.

Picking out a card that drew my eye, I peered at the image. It was a woman standing between two pillars, holding what looked like a multifaceted crystal in one hand and a book in the other. She was wearing a peculiar headdress—a circle with horns that almost looked Egyptian in style. The High Priestess. I wondered what she signified.

The bell above the door rang, and I dropped the card and glanced up. It was Boone.

He was wearing his trademark jeans, T-shirt, and tartan shirt, though this morning, the shirt was undone. As usual, his ringleted hair was falling into his eyes, and he was in desperate need of a shave.

I eyed him skeptically, more from curiosity than burning desire. He'd never been in the shop before, and I wondered what he was up to. He hadn't come to see me, had he?

"Hi," he said, smirking at me.

"Hi..." I said slowly, waiting for the punch line.

"I heard about *the incident*."

"Not you, too," I said with a moan. He'd come to rub it in! *Typical.* "I had nothing to do with that man's driving. He ended up in the creek all by himself, *thank you*."

Boone began to laugh. "It'll be the talk of Derrydun for months."

"Then someone had better hurry up and do something outrageous so they'll forget me."

"I had to put up with it for a whole year before you came along and took my crown, so I'm not in any hurry to help you along." He added a wink for good measure.

"What did you do?" I asked, narrowing my eyes. "I don't believe it."

"Bully broke Roy's leg, and I was able to calm him enough so Sean could get Roy out of the pen."

"Bully?"

"Roy's bull."

"What's so special about that?"

"Bulls are notoriously wild creatures," Boone explained. "They don't have much regard for us humans, so when they get a bee in their bonnet, it's best to run as fast as you can in the other direction. They're big bastards."

"Let me guess. You ran the wrong way?" I tilted my head to the side.

"I did, but it could've been much worse for Roy if I hadn't."

"That doesn't seem like that bad of a story," I declared. "It's not embarrassing at all."

Boone scratched his head, looking uncomfortable. "I'm not good at bein' the center of attention."

I snorted. "Seriously? Looking like that?" I gestured up and down at him. "Yeah, right. You love it."

"Are you callin' me handsome?" he asked, grinning.

"No! I..." There was no denying it. I was redder than red. Scarlet, crimson, carmine, maroon, cherry, ruby...

Boone's grin widened, and he leaned against the counter. Running his fingers over the cards I'd been studying, he glanced at me curiously.

"You found Aileen's tarot cards," he said.

"Yeah. I don't know anything about them, though." I scooped them up and began shuffling absently, finding a strange comfort in the action.

"Your mam loved these cards," he went on. "She would sit there and do a readin' every mornin'."

"Do you know anything about them?"

"A little. She would pull a few cards for me every now and then. Especially when I first came to Derrydun. She said they helped with guidance more than anythin'."

I sure could use a little of that right now, I thought as I continued shuffling.

"Would you like to draw one?" Boone asked. "I can see if it's one I remember."

I didn't see the harm in it, so I shuffled once more, then drew the card right at the top. Flipping it over, I saw it was an image of a tower surrounded by clouds with lightning bolts. The top of the structure was etched in flames, and I shivered with a foreboding sense of destruction.

"The Tower," I said, holding it up so Boone could see.

He frowned, his features troubled.

"What?" I prodded, setting the card on the counter. "Do you know what it means?"

He nodded. "The Tower looks nasty with the storm clouds and lightnin' bolts, but it can be a very nice card," he said, placing his finger on top. "The Tower must fall in order to be rebuilt. Out with the old, and in with the new."

My insides twisted, and I immediately jumped to the conclusion that read *Aileen was old, and now you're here in her place. The younger model.* That was the problem. I didn't want to pick up where she left off and become Aileen version two. I wanted to be me. I wanted to be Skye, and no one else.

I scowled and snatched up the card. "Out with the old, you say?"

Boone's expression fell, and he straightened up. "Skye, I dinna mean..."

"I know. It's just... I don't know what to think anymore. There's some kind of conspiracy going on here."

"Conspiracy?" He tilted is head to the side.

I opened my mouth, desperately wanting to discuss my wild theories with someone, but quickly closed it again. I knew how it would sound. Sky Williams would be the talk of the town for a different reason once I started flapping my gums about omens and strange coincidences.

"Is somethin' botherin' you? You can tell me, Skye," he murmured. "I won't judge."

I almost crumbled, but I ended up shaking my head. "It's just an adjustment thing. It's the same but different here, you know?"

The door opened, interrupting us at the perfect moment, and the little bell rang furiously as Mairead strode in, her boots clomping on the floor. When she saw Boone standing by the counter, her eyes widened.

"Hi, Mairead," he said, flashing her a smile. He fished around in his pocket and held out an MP3 player toward her. "Sorry I kept it for so long."

"That's okay," she muttered, taking the little player from him. She smiled shyly, then not knowing what else to say, turned away.

As she hurried out the back, I gave Boone a pointed

look.

"She loaned it to me after Aileen passed," he explained with a shrug. "It was about time I returned it."

"She made you a mixed tape," I said, raising my eyebrows.

"Aye, a playlist," he said, not getting her ulterior motive. "It was quite good. I liked it."

Rolling my eyes, I scooped up the tarot card and put it back into the deck.

"What?" he asked with a frown. Men. They were so clueless.

"You really don't see it?" I asked, thoroughly annoyed. I had no idea why I was jealous of a seventeen-year-old girl. It was all a little petty.

"See what?" Boone, however, was oblivious to just about everything it seemed.

"Never mind." I waved him off. "Did you need anything? Or were you attracted by the lure of tarot cards? You know, how cats run at the sound of a can opening?"

He laughed. "No, not really. I was just stoppin' by to see how you were gettin' on."

I raised my eyebrows slightly, my chest tightening. "I'm getting there. Slowly."

"That's good."

"I suppose."

We stared at each other awkwardly for a moment, then as Mairead reappeared, he snapped to attention.

"I better be goin', then," he said, backing toward the door. "I've got some work to do for Mary. I'll see you around."

"See ya," I replied, raising my hand in a small wave.

"Bye!" Mairead said cheerily as Boone disappeared through the door, the bell signaling his departure.

She stared after him with a dreamy expression. "He never comes into the shop," she said to me. "At least, not while I'm here."

"Have you got a crush on him?"

"*Pfft*, no." She rolled her eyes and pouted.

"You made him a playlist," I stated, making a face.

"So? He was alone after Aileen died. He still is." She sighed dramatically, and I could almost read her thoughts.

"Yeah, right," I muttered, walking over to the bookshelf and picking up a book about tarot cards. "Pull the other one."

When I went back to the cottage that afternoon, the tabby cat was waiting for me on the stoop.

"Hey, Buddy," I said, bending over to pat him on the head. I had no idea what his name was, but Buddy was universal. Kinda like calling someone mate.

Over the past week and a half, we'd become good friends. He didn't visit every evening, but more often than not, he would be waiting for me. Then he would be gone in the morning, disappearing like a ghost. I'd stopped wondering how he was getting out and accepted that like the rest of Derrydun's inhabitants, he was just as special.

Unlocking the door, I let us inside, dumped my bag on the kitchen table, and went to the freezer. Taking out my snap-frozen dinner of choice, I pierced the film on top with a fork and shoved the meal into the microwave. Leaning against the counter, I flipped open the book on tarot I'd borrowed from the shop called *Learning the Tarot*.

Buddy began doing figure eights through my legs as I skimmed the introduction. *Learning the Tarot is a complete beginner's course on learning the hidden meaning of tarot for personal guidance. These lessons teach you the fundamentals of basic readings to help you learn and practice. Fundamentals such as, how to use one card to interpret a situation, two cards in synchronicity, and how to weave multiple card spreads into a cohesive story.*

The microwave beeped, and I retrieved my meal and my bag and went upstairs with Buddy on my heels. Setting myself up on Aileen's bed, I took out the tarot deck I'd found that morning, laid out the book, and began picking at the chicken with gravy, vegetables and roast potato that I'd nuked downstairs.

Buddy curled up on the end of the bed, not in the least bit interested in the rubbery food I tortured myself with. Smart guy, that one.

"Let's see..." I said, opening the box and taking out the cards. Shuffling, I stopped when I felt like it might be right and drew the card at the top. Turning it over, I raised my eyebrows. The Tower.

It was the same card I'd chosen earlier, and I wondered if it was yet another weird sign from the spirits of Derrydun. They sure knew how to shove coincidences down my throat, after all.

"All right," I muttered. "If you want to play with me, then what do you mean."

Turning to the index, I found the page reference for the Tower and then turned back to the right place in the book.

I read the passage aloud so it would sink into my brain faster. *"When the Tower shows itself in a reading, consider it a blessing in disguise. Forceful change is being pushed on you, and though it may feel like it is happening against your will, you need to remember it's for your own good. Often, this card appears when a change has been in the air for some time, and you have resisted or ignored it. There may have been small problems arising because of this, and they are likely increasing and getting out of control. The Tower represents the Universe reminding you that you need this upheaval to run its course for your own spiritual growth.*

"Hear that, Buddy?" I said to the cat. "That sounds exactly like my life. Forceful change."

Holding up the Tower, I studied the card. Boone had said it meant 'out with the old, and in with the new.' I thought he'd been talking about Aileen passing, but maybe it was more than that. My old life had fallen apart, much like the picture of the Tower in the book. I'd lost my job, my boyfriend, my home, but now I was in Derrydun, and a whole new way of life had presented itself in an unlikely scenario. Lucky for me, I had dual citizenship.

No doubt, the part referring to the 'small problems' could be interpreted as the trio of oddities that occurred when I had decided I wanted to sell. The door to Irish Moon became stuck, the computer froze, and the real estate agent crashed his car into the creek.

It was very specific, and I found myself wanting to believe. Guidance, huh? Maybe there was more in these tarot cards than I first thought.

A loud thud broke the still air, and I jumped, my heart doing a double backflip in my chest. Even Buddy's head flew up, his eyes wide, and his irises so black hardly any green was left showing.

"The hell..." I muttered as I saw a stack of old romance novels had fallen off the nightstand onto the floor.

Scrambling off the bed, I knelt on the edge of the rug and scooped up the tattered books. Flipping them over in my hands, I snorted at the titles. *Romancing the Sheik. Desiring the Doctor. Too Hot to Handle.*

"That's a trip," I said to no one in particular. "Aileen was into Mills & Boon."

Pushing to my feet, I stumbled, the floorboard underneath the rug wobbling as I moved my weight. *What the—*

Casting the books aside, I rolled up the corner of the rug to reveal the floor underneath. Pressing my palm against each board, they were firm until I leaned heavily on the last. It shot up into the air, almost smacking me in the face. Dodging at the last moment, I grasped the plank of wood and set it aside.

Peering into the gap in the floor, I was surprised to find a book wedged in the opening. Lifting it out, I ran my fingers over the chocolate-colored cover. It was bound in leather and had been handled to the point it had softened like butter. Stroking the spine, it was silky to the touch, and it had a handmade look to it.

Curious, I opened it and began leafing through the pages. There were hand-drawn pictures, pressed flowers, scrawled handwriting, and symbols that were vaguely familiar. That one there was a pagan symbol for earth.

"Mushrooms? Wormwood, ragwort, the root of a…?" I glanced at Buddy, who was watching me from his perch on the bed. "This is weird." Turning my attention back to the book, I read incantations for protection, celebrating the waxing and waning of the moon, spells for calming and taming the weather. Even recipes for natural poultices for healing open wounds.

It was totally a spell book. The whole thing was old, crinkly, and written by hand. This wasn't any reproduction or scrapbook Aileen kept in her spare time.

As I flipped through the pages, it was becoming clearer and clearer that it had been compiled by many hands over many years. The language was strange but grew clearer the further I went until the very last pages where I was certain the handwriting belonged to Aileen. Then right at the end were dozens of blank pages.

"Who were these people?" I murmured, thinking about the woman, Mary whatshername, who lived in the ruined tower house. The White Tower. Did she have something to do with Aileen? Mary Byrne. That was it! *Mary Byrne.*

Sliding back into bed, I set the spell book on my knee and scooped the tarot cards into a neat pile. It sounded absurd, but had Aileen been a witch? Not with magical powers or anything, but...what did they call it? Wiccan?

"Buddy, I'm so confused," I said, burying my fingers into his fur. He began kneading the quilt with his claws and purring at a million miles an hour. "Not that I care one way or the other what religion Aileen followed, but..." I sighed. "No matter what I do, she's still a world away from me. Who was she? Do you know?" Buddy just blinked at me, his purring ramping up to eleven. "Even if you did know, you couldn't tell me. You're a cat." I rolled my eyes.

Flopping back onto the bed, my head hit the pillows, and I let out a frustrated cry. The puzzle only deepened the longer I was in Derrydun. If I knew who she was, then maybe I would have a chance at knowing who I was supposed to be in the wake of her death.

Something was going on here. Something just out of my reach. There was a time where coincidence became more—a tipping point—and I couldn't help feeling it was coming up fast. I would tip, but which side of the fence would I land on?

Would Derrydun claim me as its own, or would it spit me out?

CHAPTER 8

The following night, I went to Molly McCreedy's for dinner.

"Skye!" Maggie exclaimed as I walked into the homely pub. "What brings you to our fine establishment?"

She was wiping down a table just inside the door, her russet-colored curls done up into a bouncy ponytail.

"Hey. I'm after something for dinner," I replied. "I'm sick of microwave meals."

"Well, you've come to the right place. What would you like? We've got traditional lamb stew, cod and chips, steak... Anything you would like."

"Stew is fine."

Maggie nodded across the pub. "Have a seat at the bar, and I'll get the boys to fix you up."

Glancing across the room, I was surprised to find it empty other than Sean McKinnon, who was nursing a pint of beer at the bar. It was a little late, after all. Crossing the pub, I chose the stool two down from the farmer.

"You're a witch," Sean stated as I sat. "It's a fact."

My mouth fell open at the warm greeting, and I felt like

clipping him around the ear. He also smelled like a brewery, so I just flipped my hair over my shoulder and turned away.

"Aileen was related to Mary Byrne, the white witch from the tower house," he said, slurring his words. "That means she was a witch, so you're one, too."

"I really don't know if I should be offended by your stupid mouth or not," I declared. "There's no such thing as witches."

"What's so offensive about it?" His hand curled around his pint glass, and he downed a mouthful of beer. "You're a witch."

"Am not!"

"Are so!"

"Sean McKinnon!" Maggie screeched as she pushed out of the kitchen. "That's not how you talk to a lady!"

The door swung back, and I spotted Boone wiping down a bench while the cook started on my order. He glanced up just as it swung closed, and our gazes met. In that moment, electricity pinged between us, and I blinked, shaking my head.

"Gimme a beer, will you?" Sean slurred, ignoring Maggie's chastising.

"No. I'm cuttin' you off."

"Just one more, Maggie. Be a good girl."

"No. You're sloshed, Sean. No more. Get home with you before I hose you out the door." She waved furiously at him.

"Skye." He made puppy-dog eyes at me. "Would you buy me a drink? I'll pay you back."

"No way," I retorted. "I'm not enabling you, Sean McKinnon. Not after you called me a witch."

"The women in this village are nothin' but—"

"Uh!" Maggie exclaimed, interrupting him. "You be careful with that mouth of yours before I cut you off for good. Now get yourself home before my boot hits your asshole."

Sean grumbled and slipped off the barstool. Shuffling across the pub on unsteady feet, he pushed out of the door and disappeared into the night, muttering something about ungrateful women.

"Sorry about that," Maggie said to me. "He can get a little grumpy when he's had one too many."

I glanced after him and frowned. There were all kinds of drunks out there in the world. Happy drunks, fun drunks, animated drunks. Then there were the least desirable kinds. Addictive drunks, sad drunks, and abusive drunks. I wondered which one Sean was. After tonight, I was leaning toward the addicted kind considering his usual disposition. The life of the party.

"Dinner's up." Boone appeared from the kitchen and placed a giant bowl of stew in front of me.

"Thanks." I took the proffered spoon, and our fingers brushed. A zap of static electricity pinged up my arm, and I dropped the spoon onto the bar. Shaking my hand, I said, "Damn it! I thought I'd shaken the static. I was zapping everything there for a while."

Boone laughed. "Maybe Sean's right. Maybe you are a witch."

"There's no such thing, and that's mean, by the way."

"Why?" He tilted his head to the side. "You wouldn't want to be able to use magic if you could?"

I made a face and picked up the spoon. "All I'm worried about right now is food. And besides, there's no such thing as magical powers, so why bother thinking about it. If I decide to write a novel, I'll ask you for research, okay?"

"Leave the poor girl to eat in peace," Maggie shouted at Boone. "You can ask her for a kiss later."

My cheeks instantly flushed crimson, and I almost dropped the spoon again. Boone almost choked on his own spit and shoved his hand through his hair before backing away and escaping into the kitchen.

"Maggie!" I exclaimed.

"What?" She shrugged, though she wasn't able to hide the wicked grin on her face.

Embarrassed because I wouldn't have minded a full-on open-mouthed kiss from the mysterious Boone, I began shoveling stew into my mouth.

"He likes you," the bartender said in a singsong voice.

"Does not!" I exclaimed through a mouthful of potato.

"Don't be shy, Skye. There have been loads of women who've tried to capture his eye, but none have. He's a good sort, our Boone, even though he can be all mysterious. It's the trifecta if you ask me. Tall, handsome...and brooding."

"I thought it was tall, dark, and handsome?"

"Brooding is sexier." She winked.

I snorted and shoveled another spoonful of stew into my mouth so I wouldn't have to add to the conversation. Last thing I wanted was to reveal my crush on Boone. I wasn't sure why I was so embarrassed about it. I was acting like a seventeen-year-old girl. Hell, I was acting like Mairead.

Still, my curiosity won out over the fact he'd never been out with anyone. "How long did you say he's been living here?"

"About three years, I think," Maggie replied.

"And in all that time, he hasn't...*been* with anyone?"

"Nay. Not one."

"Isn't that weird?"

"It depends on how you look at it," she replied, leaning against the bar. "Some people sleep around, you know?

They don't care too much about settlin'. Others wait for somethin' more meaningful."

"And you think Boone is the latter?" I frowned.

She smirked and raised an eyebrow.

"What?" I asked, scooping out the last of the stew and licking the spoon.

"Nothin'," she said, picking up my empty bowl.

"Whatever," I declared, leaving a twenty euro note on the bar. "I'm going home before this gets any more awkward than it already is. Just let me try to remember where I parked my broomstick."

Maggie snorted and waved. "Goodnight, Skye."

Outside, the air was cool, and it felt heavenly on my flushed cheeks. Boone had not had a girlfriend in the three years he'd been living in Derrydun? *Yeah, right.* He was interested in me? *Yeah, right.* Oh, who was I kidding? The thought he might be interested in me, like in a romantic way, had my nether regions tingling.

"*Juliette...*"

The sound of a man's voice moaning somewhere in the darkness broke through my lustful thoughts, and I stepped forward without fear.

Seeing Sean McKinnon, I frowned. He'd left twenty minutes ago but hadn't made it very far at all.

He was lying in the gutter, moaning as if he were in pain. Unsure as to what I should do—in case it wasn't pain he was in but something more disturbing—I stood there watching him. He rolled over onto his back, and that was when I saw the tears staining his face.

"Sean?" I asked, taking a step toward him.

"Juliette," he said with a moan. "*Juliette...*"

"It's Skye," I murmured. "Aileen's daughter. You know,

the *witch*." Helping him to sit up, I knelt before him and placed my hands on his shoulders. "That's better, right?"

"She's gone," he muttered, then sniffed. "She's gone and left me all alone."

I wasn't sure what he was talking about, but I gathered Juliette had been his girlfriend and had broken up with him, leaving him blindsided. Now he was medicating himself with beer.

"Broken hearts suck, huh?" I said. "You know, my boyfriend broke up with me out of the blue a few days before I came here. It blows, but getting drunk and sleeping in a gutter won't help you. You'll just have one hell of a headache in the morning."

Sean was listening intently, or at least, I thought he was. He blinked every so often, signaling the lights were on, but I wasn't sure anyone was home.

Frowning, I felt a pang of sympathy for the guy. If only there were some way I could ease his pain. Taking a deep breath, I squeezed his shoulders.

"You seem harmless enough," I declared. "How about I help you home?"

"Skye?"

I glanced up at the sound of another voice and found Boone standing over us. I opened my mouth, but at the sight of him glaring at me in annoyance, I closed it again. He was giving me one hell of a dirty look, and I had no idea what I'd done to deserve it.

"What are you doin'?" he demanded.

"I found him lying in the gutter," I snapped, reacting to his uncharacteristic mood. "I didn't want to leave him here. He could get run over by a crazy driver or get sick from exposure."

"Leave him be," he said, practically pushing me aside. "I'll look after him."

Standing, I took a few steps back and scowled as Boone dragged Sean to his feet.

"Go home," Boone said irritably.

"That's all you've got to say?" My mouth fell open.

"It's dark out here," he added.

"I'm not scared of the dark." I pouted.

He didn't reply this time. Anchoring Sean against his side, he turned away and began walking in the direction of the single set of traffic lights.

"She wouldn't buy me a drink," Sean said with a slur as Boone practically carried him down the road away from me.

I watched them stumble away with a mixture of confusion and hurt.

"What did I do?" I shouted after them.

"Go home, Skye," Boone yelled back without even turning.

My heart sank as I stared after them, tears pricking at my eyes. *What did I do?* I just wanted to help. Did Boone want me to be part of this village at all? Sure didn't feel like it right now. Maybe he was starting to resent me as Aileen's daughter. He was as good as her son after all, and he got nothing in her will. Maybe I was wrong. Or maybe I was overreacting.

"Make an effort, you say!" I shouted into the darkness. "You'll always have a place here, you say! *Yeah right!*"

Kicking a rock with all my might, it skipped down the road and disappeared into Mrs. Boyle's hedge. Who was overreacting now?

"Kiss a donkey's ass!" I yelled after them.

Staring at the tarot cards on the counter at Irish Moon, I scowled. Glancing at the book I'd been using to try to decipher the meanings, I scowled even harder.

I'd drawn the Nine of Swords.

It showed a crying man with swords hanging over his head and two piercing each arm. So not what I wanted to see this morning. It reminded me of Sean McKinnon—because I couldn't refer to him as anything but his full name—and how I'd found him paralytic in the gutter last night.

The book told me it was to do with being alone in the world, and the swords hanging down represented vulnerability and an uncertain fate hanging over one's head. I felt a lot like that person depicted on the card this morning, especially after Boone's attitude last night.

The bell jingled above the door as Mairead walked in, and I almost jumped out of my skin. She clomped across the shop, her earphones stuck in her ears, and disappeared out the back.

The bell jingled again, and I glanced up. This time, Boone walked in, and I rolled my eyes and turned back to the tarot cards.

"I just wanted to let you know—"

"What. *Ever*," I declared, not even looking at him.

"Skye."

"That's my name, don't wear it out."

"You're mad at me," he stated.

"*Duh.*"

The way he'd glared at me last night still cut, and the command he'd barked—*go home, Skye*—grated my raw heart. I didn't expect him to act that way, and I'd only been trying to help. It wasn't like I was going to take advantage of a drunk man or vice versa. Sean couldn't even walk without being propped up, let alone go in for a grope. What was the big deal? Maybe I'd broken some sort of unspoken Derrydun bro code.

"Skye..."

"I'm not in the mood, Boone," I said thinly. "Not right now."

He sighed and shuffled from foot to foot. When he finally got I wasn't going to give him any more one-syllable words, he turned and strode from the shop. The bell dinged violently, and the door slammed shut. Lifting my head, I watched him power across the road and disappear into Mary's Teahouse.

Mairead appeared in front of me, and I glanced away.

"What's going on with you two?" she asked, narrowing her eyes.

I sighed dramatically. "I found Sean McKinnon in the gutter last night and tried to help him, but Boone got his knickers in a twist over it."

"Ah, he's always takin' Sean home," she explained.

"Well, he must have a crush on the guy because he didn't like sharing," I said sullenly. I knew I was acting like a spoilt child, but the one-liners kept coming.

"Nah, he's not that way inclined," Mairead said, sounding offended.

"Oh, that's right," I said with a smile. "You've got a crush on him."

"Have not!" She stamped her foot. Like, she actually raised her boot off the ground and thumped it onto the floorboards.

"You're too easy." I laughed and shook my head.

At that precise moment, the serene and sunny morning was split apart by the musical sound of flutes blaring over a loudspeaker. I glanced at Mairead. Then the soft crooning of a female voice began singing, "Far across the distance..."

"Is that...*Celine Dion?*" I asked, screwing up my face.

"Holy shite!" Mairead declared, pressing her nose up against the window. "He's gonna jump!" Then she threw open the door and ran outside.

Leaping off the stool, I rounded the counter and followed Mairead outside. A little group of people had begun to gather around Molly McCreedy's, and I followed their stunned pointing, wondering what was going on.

Shielding my eyes from the glare of the sun, my mouth dropped open as I saw Sean McKinnon sitting on the thatched roof, holding a little wireless speaker high in the air, swaying side to side to the music, and singing at the top of his lungs. Needless to say, he wasn't any good.

Standing beside Maggie, who was watching on with her arms crossed over her chest, I realized he was drunk. He'd have to be to sit up there and play a Celine Dion song at that volume.

"It's not even lunchtime, and he's drunk as a skunk," I said. "What's gotten into him?"

"It's the anniversary of his wife's death," Maggie replied. "It's been four years, but every day is the same for him. She's not here, and he barely hangs on."

Thinking back to last night, it all made sense. He'd been sitting in the gutter, muttering a woman's name. *Juliette.* I thought he'd been dumped, but she'd died. It was so much worse.

I frowned, my shoulders sinking. "The poor guy. Is anyone going to get him down?"

"Ah, here comes Boone with the ladder now."

Turning, I saw Boone's curly hair come into view. He appeared from behind Mary's Teahouse carrying a long ladder, which he leaned against the side of the pub.

Ignoring the gaggle of onlookers, he climbed up onto the roof and edged over to Sean.

"Boone!" Sean exclaimed at the top of his lungs. "You're Boone!"

"That's right," he replied, reaching for the speaker. "What are you doin' up here?"

"My heart will go on," he said, attempting to snatch the speaker out of Boone's hands. "I've got to let her know. It's our tradition, you know."

"I know, but she's gone, Sean. Juliette's gone."

Glancing nervously at Maggie, I was feeling rather foolish standing out here watching a full-grown man fall apart. Thinking about the Nine of Swords, I was beginning to understand its message hadn't been for me. It was for Sean McKinnon.

"No!" Sean roared, hurling the speaker off the roof. It hit the road and smashed into a million pieces, and the song cut off.

"C'mon," Boone said, clapping his hand on the man's shoulder. "Let's get down, and we can talk about it."

"No, no, no, no..." Sean cried before bursting out into full-blown sobs.

Boone slapped his free hand on Sean's other shoulder. The movement set the farmer off, and he dragged the younger man into a full-on ugly cry hug.

Boone's gaze met mine, and I frowned. I'd overreacted this morning when he'd come in. I had no idea what he'd wanted to say—maybe he'd been trying to tell me he got Sean home safely—but I wasn't sure it mattered. Not after the way I'd dismissed him. Seeing him up on that roof... Boone was good people.

"Mairead, let's go back inside," I said, tugging on the girl's sleeve.

"*But*—"

"No buts," I scolded her. "This isn't a sideshow. Leave the poor guy in peace."

"You sound more and more like Aileen the longer you stay here," she grumbled, stomping into the shop.

"I'm choosing to ignore that," I declared, following her inside.

Glancing over my shoulder one last time, I saw Boone helping Sean down the ladder. Yeah, he was good people.

CHAPTER 9

Sean McKinnon was the talk of Derrydun for days after the incident on the roof of Molly McCreedy's. I didn't want to be relieved they were no longer talking about me and the real estate agent crashing his car into the creek, not considering what it took to have it knocked from the top spot, but I was. Just a little.

Maggie convinced me not to worry about the guy, so I didn't. Sean had become the town drunk in the wake of his wife's death, and it seemed like that was the way it was. I didn't agree with it at all. Something was going to happen, and my gut told me it wouldn't be anything nice. Not unless he stopped drinking himself into an early grave.

The next morning, I drew the Tower again from Aileen's deck of golden tarot cards. Relieved it wasn't the Nine of Swords, I took it as a sign things were going back to normal. I'd deviated from the track for a few days, and now I was back on the path to rebuilding. To my surprise, I was actually getting into the whole tarot thing, so much so that I'd put money into the till for the book I'd borrowed and started scribbling notes in the margins. Maybe, just maybe, this was what would connect me with my absentee dead mother. The mother who was still a mystery with her crystal shop and weird spell book under the floorboards.

Still upset with how Boone had spoken to me, I spent my day off from Irish Moon as far away from Derrydun as my legs would take me. Without a car—I'd returned the rental weeks ago—I was limited to my own two feet to get me around.

I went to see the tower house first.

Sean McKinnon had said Aileen was related to the woman who lived here, Mary Byrne, who was burned at the stake for allegedly being a witch. I didn't know about that, but it was still an absurd notion. When the ruins didn't reveal any more secrets than it had the first day I'd explored, I set off on the path that led toward the forest on the other side of the hill.

I'd never been this far from Derrydun before. The further my feet took me, the more I felt like there were a thousand and one pairs of eyes just outside my field of vision. They were all watching me, the strange Australian girl who still felt like an interloper, tread through the woods.

Brilliant green ferns blanketed the ground between moss-encrusted trees, and the pink and red of wild fuchsia broke up the earthy tones. It was beautiful out here, but I felt exposed. Shivering, I wrapped my arms around myself and glanced back and forth nervously.

It wasn't long before a clearing opened up in front of me, and my mouth opened in awe as I saw a giant gnarled tree towering over the forest. Approaching, I studied the leaves and branches trying to figure out what kind it was. It reminded me of the hawthorn in the village, and I decided it was another. A really old one by the looks of it.

It was *massive*. It would take at least two or three of me to encircle the trunk with open arms, though now I was up close, it wasn't that much taller than the woods around it. Short and squat for its trunk size was an apt description.

A low growl hummed behind me in the stillness, and I spun around, my heart twisting with fright. A gray and white wolf stood in the center of the clearing, its fangs bared in a menacing snarl. Its golden gaze was locked directly on me, and it looked hungry. The saliva dripping from razor sharp fangs kind of hungry.

Stumbling, my back hit the trunk of the hawthorn. Where had the beast come from? No one had warned me about wolves... Boone hadn't... There was no time to debate why.

Watching the wolf, I knew if I fled, it would give chase, and there was no way I would be able to outrun it. It was twice the size of a German Shepard, and its teeth were longer and sharper than I'd ever seen. I was so screwed.

My palms grasped the gnarled trunk of the hawthorn as I stared it down. I was going to be eaten on my day off. Just my luck.

"What are you waiting for?" I whispered. "You know I can't run."

Its haunches tensed as it readied itself to leap, and I flung my arms up in front of my face to protect myself. Then the beast launched itself forward, and I screamed.

In the moment right before death, wasn't your life supposed to flash before your eyes? That was what everyone said, but I didn't see anything. Just the glowing eyes of the wolf as it came right for me, its sharp teeth dripping with saliva. Boy, he was sure hungry today.

Just as I was certain I was going to become the main course—scared Australian girl du jour—a flash of red streaked through the clearing and slammed into the side of the wolf. The beast let out a surprised yelp and tumbled to the side.

Scrambling backward, I gasped as I saw a russet-colored fox sinking its teeth into the wolf's neck. What the hell was going on here?

The fox clamped down its jaws and shook, but the wolf was stronger. It rolled and flung the little creature across the clearing before leaping toward it. Its teeth chomped down on the little guy's back leg, causing him to yelp in pain.

A pang of despair tore through my heart at the sight of my rescuer—no matter how odd a rescuer it was—and I hesitated. I knew I should run while the going was good, but I couldn't leave the fox behind. *Damn, my bleeding heart.*

Looking frantically around the clearing, I spied a fallen branch. Like a strange power had overcome me, I pushed off the hawthorn, leaped forward, grasped the end of the thick stick, and held it high.

"Hey!" I shouted at the wolf. "Let him go!"

It raised its head, its jaws letting go of the fox. Its eyes were rabid, its teeth were red with blood, and it began to growl menacingly as its attention fixed back onto its original target. *Me.*

"Just try it," I said, snarling. "You had better run before I whack you back into last century, you bastard. Don't think I won't, or you'll get a nasty surprise."

Two things happened at that moment. The first was that the wolf leaped at me. The second was me swinging the stick with all the strength I could muster. It sounded like a fruitless endeavor, smacking a giant wolf around the head with a pointy little stick, but it was my only choice.

My dad always used to tell me off for swinging sticks around, saying it was all fun and games until someone lost an eye. Needless to say, no one had ever lost one...until today.

The stick collided with the wolf's head, and it yelped in surprise as a point speared right into its left eyeball. I felt a sickening *pop* ricochet up the branch and through my arm, and I almost hurled on the spot.

The wolf whined as it scurried backward, and the stick pulled out of its eye, leaving a gush of blood in its wake. Howling, the beast shook its head and took off, leaping through the trees and running for its life.

"Holy shit," I exclaimed, still holding onto the stick. "I took out its eye. I'm going to puke."

A shuffling sound drew my attention back to the clearing. Glancing at the fox, I wasn't sure what to do. It was lying where the wolf had left it, blood matting its hind leg. Should I help it?

Frowning, I knew it was a wild animal and probably wouldn't let me near at all. It stared at me for a long time and then rose to its feet. It yipped once as though it was beckoning me to leave and slunk away, melting into the surrounding forest.

After a moment, everything seemed to come back to life. Birds began chirping, insects buzzed, and the foreboding I'd sensed right before the wolf appeared lifted. Still, I didn't stick around to revel in my victory, which had been dumb luck and nothing else.

Dropping the bloodied stick, I turned and sprinted back the way I'd come and didn't stop until I'd locked myself in the cottage.

That night, I didn't sleep at all. Buddy didn't show up, so I was alone with my fear. Every sound was a wolf coming to eat me, and every shadow held a pair of glowing golden eyes, which was absurd since I poked one of them out. Like full on popped it like a grape.

Squirming, I buried underneath the quilt and waited for the sunrise.

Mary's Teahouse wasn't my first choice for breakfast the next morning, but I didn't have an alternative. It was the only establishment in a ten-mile radius that served hot food —that didn't need to be microwaved—before nine a.m.

Opening the door, I shuffled inside, the frilly pink decor assaulting my eyes. The little cafe was empty, and when I appeared, Mary Donnelly herself emerged looking a sight more cheery than I felt after my sleepless night. I was sure I looked like I had two black eyes, no matter how much concealer I'd piled on before leaving the cottage.

Mary was a sweet, little, old lady in her seventies, who'd run the teahouse for over fifty years. According to Maggie, Mary had never married, nor had any children. Instead, she took on the village as her surrogate family. She was well worn into Derrydun like she was part of the furniture, or so the saying went. She was also Irish through and through.

"Good mornin', Skye," she said cheerfully, smoothing down her pink and white frilly apron.

"Hi, Mary," I replied, flopping down at a table in the center of the room.

"Are you all right?" the old woman asked, instantly picking up on my mood. "Would you like to talk about it?"

I froze. For the first time, I could understand her accent. The handful of times I'd greeted her out in the street, she'd spoken with such a thick Irish brogue, I couldn't make out a single word. Usually, I just smiled and nodded, but today, she was clear as a bell. It was like someone had come along and flipped the switch in my brain labeled 'Irish assimilation.'

"Are there wolves in Ireland?" I asked.

"Wolves? No, not anymore," Mary replied, raising her eyebrows. "They were all hunted and killed a hundred years ago."

"Oh..." Then what did I see yesterday? A hallucination?

"How are things goin' with Irish Moon?"

"Okay. Well, great actually. I finally understand how everything works. The books, the tax thing, the ordering. Mairead knows that place inside out. I don't know what I would've done without her."

"She's a strange one that Mairead," Mary said, clucking her tongue. "What with her black clothes and her sickly skin. That girl needs a good feed."

I snorted, trying to hold in my laughter. "She's a Goth, Mary."

"A what?" The old woman made a face. "I can't keep up with the kids nowadays. A Goth, you say? I thought they were barbarians from Germany."

I covered my mouth with my hand and picked up a menu with the other.

"And how are you after your mother's passin'?" Mary added, once her confusion over Mairead's fashion choices had subsided.

I made a face, and Mary grasped my hand. Her skin was cool and soft, and the moment she touched me, I felt a zap.

"You don't have to step into your mother's shoes, Skye," she said kindly as if she'd read my thoughts. "No one expects you to."

"It feels like it. I'm living in her house. I'm running her shop..."

"They're yours now." She smiled sweetly. "Run the shop how you see fit. Decorate the cottage to your likin'."

I stared at her in shock. But those were Aileen's things. *That she left to me.* Mary was right.

"Don't worry about the wildlife," she added for good measure. "The worst around here is the odd deer or fox, and they're more afraid of you than you are of them."

"I'm going to trust you," I said. "Don't make me regret it."

"You cheeky thing!" she exclaimed with a laugh. "Let me fix you something for breakfast. Let me see. Tea, toast, scrambled eggs, and bacon. Oh, and tomato and a sausage. A big fat one. That'll fill you right up. Nothin' better than a little comfort food when you're feeling down."

"And fill out my hips and ass," I retorted.

"Nonsense. You're flat as a tack." She waved her hand at me and shuffled toward the kitchen, leaving me to my own devices.

Glancing down at my boobs, which weren't *that* flat, I thought about what she'd said about the local wildlife. No wolves in Ireland? It sure looked like one to me even though I'd never seen one in the flesh before. They didn't roam Australia, either. The worst we had to worry about back home were the little critters—snakes and spiders—who knew how to hide and slither into tight spaces.

The chair across from mine scraped back, and I glanced up from my boob assessment as Boone sat down. I frowned and didn't say a word. Truthfully, after yesterday's excitement, I'd forgotten why I was mad at him in the first place. He'd been snippy, but it seemed trivial after almost being eaten alive by a creature that was supposed to be extinct on the shores of Ireland.

"Skye, I, uh..." He rubbed his hand along his jaw,

scratching his stubbly chin. "I'm sorry, for the way I spoke to you the other night."

I shrugged. "It seems like such a small thing now."

"Are you okay?" His brow furrowed, and he looked me over like he was seeing me for the first time. Flat boobs and all.

"I, um..." I glanced out the window, my gaze latching onto the green treetops. How was I supposed to explain a fox—which was a quarter of the size of the wolf—attacking a predator who was about to eat me? This place was trying its darnedest to send me to the loony bin.

"Skye..." He hesitated, then pursed his lips together.

"What?" I asked, straightening up. He wanted to tell me something but thought better of it. It was written all over his face, and now I knew I really wanted to know.

"Nothing, I..." He met my gaze and smiled. "Do you accept my apology? Put me out of me misery."

"I forgive you," I said without hesitation. With big, sad, puppy-dog eyes like his, how could I not?

"Good. I'm glad." He scraped his chair back and stood. "I'll be seein' you."

I nodded, and he walked across the teahouse, limping slightly. He was favoring his left leg, his gait significantly off. Well, not a great deal, but enough that I noticed it.

"Boone?" I called out after him. "Are you all right? You're limping."

He stopped and threw me a glance over his shoulder. "Yeah, I'm all right. I banged me knee, is all."

He didn't look it, but I wasn't in the mood to press. Mr. Mysterious could have this one.

"Oh, and be careful if you go walkin' in the woods," he added. "Roy found some tracks around the field this mornin'."

"Tracks?" I asked, shivering. It was much too late to heed his warning, but I didn't let on.

"Aye, big ones."

"What is it?"

"A wild dog maybe. Or a fox. I don't know. I'll be out in the fields until we can trap it, or until we're sure it's gone."

I screwed my face up as an image of the wolf that had stalked me popped into my mind's eye.

"I'll see you around," Boone said before disappearing outside.

Mary reappeared the moment the door closed. Setting down a plate full of the greasiest hot breakfast I'd ever seen, she stared after Mr. Mysterious.

"Oh, Boone isn't stayin'?" the old woman bemoaned. "What a shame. He's a good boy."

"Yeah," I muttered. "He is."

CHAPTER 10

That night, as Buddy kept me company, I fell asleep to the sound of wind howling through the trees outside. Plagued with dreams of wolves, I tossed and turned until I slipped into a deep slumber.

When dawn finally broke, I was covered in a thin sheen of sweat, and my head was stuffed with cotton wool. I'd slept but not really. A heavy burden was over my heart, and my body had become twisted in the quilt, my feet trapped.

Ugh, I was all hot and sticky. I kicked, trying to shift the uncomfortable weight and turned over, but it didn't budge. Lifting my head, my eyes cracked open, sleep still clogging my head. That was when I saw a lump at the end of the bed. A very large, man-shaped lump.

Now completely awake, I screamed, scrambling up the bed. It was Boone. A very *naked* Boone.

He started, his head shooting up, and when he saw me, he rolled and fell off the end of the bed, hitting the floor with a thud. Scrambling to his feet, his face turned a deep shade of crimson.

"Oh, shit," he cursed, covering his junk with his hands. "Oh, *cac*."

"*Cac?*" I yelled. "I'll give you bloody Irish *cac!*"

Grabbing the lamp on the bedside table, I pushed up onto my knees and swung it with all my might. The plug popped out of the wall, and the shade barely missed Boone's face, but the cord came around and whipped him directly on his bare ass.

He howled in pain and retreated across the room.

"*Pervert!*" I shrieked.

"Let me explain," he said, holding up his hands and leaving nothing to the imagination.

"Explain? What's there to explain?" I shouted, trying not to look at his *you-know-what*. "You were asleep on the end of my bed...*naked!*" I swung the lamp at him again, barely missing his head. "You're still standing there. *I can see your meat and two veg!*"

"Oh, *cac*," he said again. "I didn't mean for you to find out this way..."

"Find out what? That you're a pervert, who sneaks into women's homes butt naked?"

"Yesterday... That was me!" he exclaimed, covering himself with a cushion.

The lamp almost fell from my grasp.

He shied away. "The wolf in the forest..."

I wasn't following. The wolf was his pet, and he was taking it for a walk? Was he training it to maul innocent women to death? I knew Derrydun was weird but homicidal? That was a new one I didn't see coming.

"That wolf is yours?" I asked, screwing up my face. "It almost ripped me apart!"

"Nay," he said, shaking his head. "The fox..." He seemed

to be having trouble getting his story straight, which wasn't helping my mood.

"Get out," I demanded. "Get out of my house before I call the police."

"Nay! I was the fox! *I was the fox...*"

I screwed up my face. "You were the fox?"

"Think about it," he pleaded. "Yesterday you saw me limpin'. You asked me if I was all right."

I stared at him, my thoughts going back to yesterday morning at Mary's Teahouse. He said he'd banged his knee. *He banged his knee.*

"You were the fox?" I said, raising my eyebrows. "*You?*"

"Skye, you've gotta believe me."

"I don't *gotta* do anything," I declared. "What are you doing in my house? How did you get in?"

"Buddy..." he began.

"Father O'Donegal's tabby cat?" I made a face. "A house cat can unlock doors now?"

"Nay... I..."

"Spit it out, Boone."

"I..." He stared at the floor, his shoulders sinking. "There's too much to explain. I can't tell you here... They've already come lookin'."

"What the hell are you talking about?" I exclaimed. "My patience is wearing real thin, you know."

His gaze met mine, and there was desperation in his eyes that almost frightened me. "Go to the hawthorn in the forest. Go there, and I will tell you everythin'. I'll wait as long as it takes."

"You want me to go into the forest, *alone*, with you?" I scoffed. "Yeah, right. I'm not dumb. I'm not going back out there!"

"Please," he pleaded, looking forlorn.

It was such a genuine expression I almost caved, but how did you believe a naked man who magically appeared in your room telling wild stories about being a fox who saved your life? Anyway, I ended up saving the fox from being torn apart, *so there!*

I screwed my eyes shut and let out an annoyed cry. "Get out!"

"Please, Skye. You'll be safe. The wolf is gone and won't be coming back anytime soon. I made sure."

"I said *get out!*" This time, I hurled the lamp at him. He ducked just in time, and it crashed against the wall, the globe shattering.

"*Cac!*" he exclaimed, fleeing from the bedroom. A second later, the cushion flew back into the room, and the sound of his feet slapping on the stairs echoed through the cottage.

Downstairs, the door slammed closed. Padding over to the window, I pressed my forehead against the glass and peered at the garden below. I expected to see a flesh-colored streak sprinting across the yard, but I shied away when I saw Buddy leap over the fence and disappear into the bushes.

Rubbing my eyes, I decided he was just on an early morning adventure collecting mice. He hadn't been here when I found Boone. He'd never stuck around in the morning, anyway. Boone wasn't Buddy...was he?

Snorting at the absurd thought, I turned away from the window. The longer I stood there, the more my mood simmered. Thinking of all the strange coincidences that had happened since arriving in Derrydun, my willpower began to break down. The strange man who'd been at Aileen's wake at Molly McCreedy's. The trifecta of weird that had stopped me from selling Irish Moon. Sean McKinnon calling me a witch. The escape artist known as Buddy. The wolf almost chomping my face off, and the fox that had fought it off. The wolf that was supposed to be extinct.

I swallowed hard and curled my freezing toes into the fluffy rug underfoot. What if Boone was right? I didn't want to utter the word 'supernatural' but what if...

I shook my head and stomped down the hall into the bathroom. It was stupid. This whole thing was stupid.

Boone was a pervert. A complete and utter closet weirdo. Wasn't he?

CHAPTER 11

It wasn't every morning someone woke up to find a naked Irishman asleep on the end of their bed. Well, not unless there had been lots of drinking the night before. Considering I'd been sober since Aileen's funeral, finding Boone that morning had been super creepy.

I didn't want to meet him at the hawthorn, not after whipping his bare ass with the lamp cord, but he had an awful lot of explaining to do. I also didn't want to go back into the forest to the clearing where the wolf almost had me for lunch, either. It was bad news.

But curiosity won against fear, and I found myself slinking down the path toward the giant hawthorn tree.

I left Mairead in charge of Irish Moon, telling her I had some errands to run, and she was happy enough to handle things on her own for a while. Ever since the real estate agent crashed his car into the creek, she'd been happy as a clam. She ought to be. Her summer job was secure, and the clueless Australian paid her more than minimum wage because the money felt funny here.

My boots crunched underfoot as I made my way

through the forest, the path curling through the thickening trees. Listening, I tried to make out the individual sounds around me, trying to figure out if I was being followed or not. It didn't help that I didn't know what I should be listening for in the first place. Everything sounded like a predator out here. Branches snapped and leaves rustled all around me, but it could just be the deer Mary from the teahouse had told me about. She said they roamed around Derrydun.

Hell. Should I be worried about being poked up the backside by a pair of antlers? Glancing around, I couldn't see any rabid deer in the vicinity, but that didn't mean they weren't hanging around.

It wasn't long before I came up to the clearing. I could see the break in the woods ahead, and my heart began to thump wildly. Deciding to sneak, I stepped off the path and ducked behind a tree, then darted to the next, getting closer each time. Ferns brushed against my shins as I lingered, and I was pretty sure my covert operation wasn't as covert as I intended. I knew nothing about the wilderness, and it showed in the racket I was making hiding in the underbrush.

Concealing myself behind the closest trunk, I leaned around and searched for Boone. I sucked in a sharp breath as I saw him pacing back and forth in front of the hawthorn, fully clothed this time. *Thank God.*

Yesterday, I wanted to check him out, and maybe let him kiss me, but that was before he flashed me in my bedroom. Ugh, I was never going to be able to keep a guy interested long enough to fall in love. *Typical!*

He stopped and glanced around, sensing—or hearing—my approach.

"Skye?" he called out.

Sighing, I knew I'd been made, so I stepped out from behind the tree and into the clearing.

"You'd better not have lured me out here so you can chop me up into little pieces," I declared.

His gaze shot to mine, and he swallowed hard. "Skye, I'm sorry, I didn't want you to find out like this..."

"Start talking," I demanded, not wanting to entertain any groveling.

"I was in my cat shape, and I fell asleep by accident," he declared. "After the wolf bit me leg, it took time to heal, and it always drains me energy. I didn't mean to frighten you."

"Wait. The wolf?" I scowled. "What's a cat shape?"

"I made a promise to Aileen that I would protect you," he said, rushing through his explanation. "She asked me to help you, so I have been helpin' best I can, but I couldn't tell you. She said you had to find out for yourself, but I guess it's a moot point now."

"What are you talking about?" I exclaimed. "Slow the hell down, and just say it already!"

Boone took a deep breath and declared, "You are the last of the Crescent Witches, Skye."

I scoffed and rolled my eyes. "Yeah, right."

"You are. The Crescent Witches are the most powerful coven there ever was," he said defiantly. "Aileen bound your powers when you were a babe to protect you. Robert told me he unbound them when he visited you in Australia."

"He what?" I exclaimed.

"He unbound your powers."

I thought about it for a long moment, then remembered the lawyer's solid gold pen and his all-around weirdness.

"He zapped me with his pen!" I was outraged, and then I dissolved into fits of laughter as I realized how stupid this all was. A little Irish lawyer had gone all the way to Australia to zap me with his magical golden pen to unlock my hereditary witch juju. Next Boone would be telling me Robert O'Keeffe was a leprechaun!

"He zapped me with his magical pen, and now you're telling me I'm a witch," I exclaimed. "But not a plain one, a real badass."

"Yeah." He looked totally serious, and I snorted.

"And you can turn into a tabby cat?"

"Not just a tabby cat," he grumbled. "I can be lots of things."

"I hope so because that's really lame! *Hello, my name is Boone the badass, and I can turn into a house cat.*" I snorted again and burst out into peals of laughter. "Lame!"

"Hey!"

"You're mental." I threw my hands into the air. "Completely off the charts. I've heard some pretty creative excuses in my time but shapeshifting and witches? You could've said you'd slept walked, and I might've believed you and not pressed charges, but this?" I snorted and turned away, determined to put as much distance between Boone and me as possible. This was not the scenario I'd pictured when I'd decided I wanted to see his bare ass. Not at all.

"Wait!" he called out. "What if I can prove it to you?"

I hesitated.

"I can show you... I can..."

I glanced over my shoulder. He was standing in the middle of the clearing, his hands curled into tight fists.

"The fox is me familiar," he murmured. "It's the first shape I remember bein'."

"Then show me," I challenged. I faced him, knowing he would choke and reveal his lie. "Show me, and prove it."

He shucked off his jacket, and I recoiled.

"I don't want to see your bits again!" I shrieked.

"Wait..." he murmured. "Watch..."

Boone kicked off his boots and stood completely still. Then something strange began to happen. His body began to shrink, his face and arms sprouted russet-colored fur, and his nose began to grow. The sound of snapping bones echoed across the clearing, and I flinched as his arms twisted and his elbow began to bend at an unnatural angle.

"Boone..." I said uneasily, but it didn't make any difference.

My mouth fell open as he disappeared among his clothes, and a bushy tail shook free of his jeans. Then another almighty shake as he shucked off his T-shirt.

"Holy Mother of..."

A red and white fox stood where Boone was a moment ago, his back paws buried in the leaf litter. Swishing his tail back and forth, he let out a yip as if to say *I told you so.*

Kneeling in the leaf litter, I stared into his honey-colored eyes in shock. I reached out with a shaking hand, and he head butted my palm gently. His fur was wiry to the touch, but his black-tipped ears were soft as silk.

"Holy..." I whispered. "I'm going mad. This isn't real. This..."

Boone nuzzled against my hand and yipped.

"You were limping yesterday... You were... You saved me from the wolf!" I covered my face with my hands. "Oh, God. What if I hadn't poked its eye out with that stick?"

Boone flicked his tail back and forth.

"And... All that time you were the cat? You were Buddy?" Remembering the first night he'd appeared, my cheeks turned red. Oh, God. I'd held up his tail and checked out his balls. His big, tabby cat balls.

He yipped again, this time dancing from foot to foot.

"You're embarrassing the hell out me right now," I grumbled. "You didn't look when I was changing, did you?"

He tilted his fox head to the side.

I gasped. "I'm going to smack you one if you did!"

Rising off his haunches, Boone circled back to his pile of clothing and glanced at me, indicating he was going to change back. I didn't want to see him morph unnaturally again, so I turned around.

He'd changed into a fox! I had so many questions I wanted to fire off at him, but most of all, I was surprised by the fact I wasn't freaking out. I mean, I should probably be running back toward the village screaming like a banshee right about now, but I'd just cuddled a fox. A fox that was Boone—the hot, mysterious Irishman. Oh, God, I'd seen his *thing*.

"You can turn around now."

"Are you decent?" I asked, covering my eyes with my hands.

"I'm decent."

I shuffled around, still hiding behind my hands. "Swear it!"

"I swear."

Peeking through my fingers, I saw Boone was Boone again, and he was fully dressed. Sighing, I dropped my hands away. I'd seen more than enough unexpected doodle for one day.

"No one must know," he said, watching me closely. He was waiting for me to run away screaming, but I hadn't moved an inch. *Yet*.

"That's convenient," I said dryly.

"Skye, you mustn't say a word."

"Why?"

"Witches are being hunted," he replied, his tone gravely

serious. "It's not all rainbows and sunshine out there. Darkness looms..."

"Witches are being hunted? What for?" I held up my hands and stared at my palms. "I'm not special. I can't do magic spells or whatever. I'm just a woman. A plain, ordinary woman."

"You can't tell me strange things haven't been happenin' to you since you arrived," he said, sitting beside me. "Think about it, Skye."

The day of the funeral, the hawthorn sapling on top of the hill had shuddered and leaned toward me like I was a magnet. The air had been still, and no gusts of wind had whipped it. The man at Molly McCreedy's with the blue skin and pointy teeth. The wolf stalking me in this very spot. Then there was the night I found Sean McKinnon by the side of the road. I'd placed my hands on his shoulders, and he'd seemed to calm down at my touch. Was that why Boone was so mad at me? Had I used some kind of magic to soothe the man's sorrow?

"Sean McKinnon... That was..." I glanced at Boone in shock. "No... That's just coincidence!"

"It was your magic. I felt it clear as day."

"Then why were you so pissed at me?" I exclaimed.

"You need to be careful," he replied. "When you use your magic, you become a beacon."

"I revealed myself? To who?" My gaze shifted to the forest, the shadows lengthening and growing eyes.

"Nobody. I've been watchin'. Though the wolf... I don't think he knew about you. You poked him with a branch from the hawthorn and took his eye. He won't come back anytime soon."

"The magical hawthorn?" I asked, remembering how

everybody was fond of telling the story about them being fairy trees.

"Aye, the hawthorn."

I scowled, my thoughts scattered. None of it made sense, and I felt like I was on the brink of a mental breakdown.

"This whole time, you've been looking out for me?" I peered at him, not sure how to take it. I mean, learning about my absent mother was a lot to deal with when I'd first arrived, but now I'd poked the eye out of an unnatural wolf with a magical stick, seen Boone turn into a fox, and heard his wild story about me being some sort of Crescent Witch... I was going mad. I actually needed a straitjacket, *stat*.

He nodded. "I made a promise to your mam."

"What else did she say?"

"She said you didn't know about your heritage and that fate would draw you here. Without anyone to guide you, she asked me to watch over you."

"Fate?" I asked. "What does that mean?"

"When your mother passed, there were no Crescent Witches left to protect Derrydun and the hawthorns, so fate drew you back to your ancestral home. I don't know much about it, but I'm beginnin' to believe it has conspired to keep you here."

Now that he mentioned it, everything began to fall apart the moment Aileen died. I'd lost my job, my boyfriend dumped me, and Robert showed up with his magic pen with its terms and conditions. Then when I tried to sell Irish Moon, the door became stuck, the computer had a glitch, and the real estate agent crashed his car into the creek.

"Son of a..." Drawing in a deep breath, I began to understand something very important. "That's why she left Dad and me, wasn't it? To protect me from all this?"

"She never really said," Boone replied. "Not outright, but I believe it to be so."

I shook my head in disbelief, my heart aching. "I hated her for so long..."

"You didn't know," he argued. "*You didn't know*."

"I still don't know," I shot back. "I... This is a lot to deal with Boone. I don't..." *I don't know if I believe you.* I believed he was a shapeshifter—that was hard to deny—but all the things he'd said about me?

"Now that you know, you can ask me anythin' you want," he said. "I'll tell you everythin' I can."

A million things flew into my mind, and I blurted out the first thing that popped into it. "What have the hawthorns got to do with it? Are the stories you told me true? Are they really doorways?"

"They are," he replied, confirming my suspicions. "They guard the doorways to the fae realm, but they were sealed a thousand years ago. Nothin' can get in or out. Now the hawthorns are safe havens."

"Safe havens?"

Boone nodded. "They are a shield for words and magic. That's why we can talk freely here. This tree was where the Crescents have practiced their magic for centuries. Or so Aileen told me."

"Why was the way to the fae realm sealed off? Do you know what it's like there?"

"It's a long story."

I scowled, desperate to know everything about this new world I was supposed to be part of. "Don't you want to tell me?"

"No, it's not that. It's just as I said. It's a long story. Perhaps another time." He smiled a sad smile and glanced up at the tree. "The doorways are never openin' again, so there's nothin' to worry about. There are creatures who still try to get in, and that's why the witches protect the trees. When the doorways were sealed, a lot of fae were trapped here. Being cut off from magic, they've become twisted."

"They need magic to survive," I mused. "That's why witches are hunted."

Boone shrugged, giving away the fact he wasn't telling me the whole story. I would get it out of him eventually. Something else was in play here, and it worried him. Not enough to warn me away though, so the lack of urgency calmed me a little.

"Where did you come from?" I asked after a moment. "Mairead said you just showed up one day."

"I don't know," he replied.

"What do you mean you don't know?"

"Before this place, I don't remember anythin'. My first memory is runnin' as a fox through the forest. Then I was flyin' as a gyrfalcon, and then I crashed to earth. They were chasin' me... It was your mam who found me right here in this clearin'."

"Who was chasing you?"

He was silent for a long time. Finally, he turned his head and smiled. "That's a story for another time."

So much evasion. Digging my hands into the leaf litter, I picked through the sticks, breathing in the heavy scent of disturbed earth.

I thought over all the peculiar things that had happened since I arrived, and I knew Boone was right. About everything. It was farfetched, fantastical, and completely bonkers, but it was real. There was just too much evidence not to believe. Seeing the guy you had the hots for morph into a bright red fox was pretty solid proof, after all.

"Boone?" I asked, breaking up the leaf in my fingers.

"Yeah?"

"Robert's a leprechaun, isn't he?"

"I suppose he is," he replied. "He's never confirmed nor denied, but he likes to drop hints. He's definitely not human, that I know."

I turned my attention back to the leaf in my hand. If I was supposed to be this badass Crescent Witch, then how was I supposed to use my magic? Where was it? Stuffed if I knew because I didn't feel any different.

"Boone?"

"Yeah?"

"What do I do now?"

He shrugged, which wasn't any help at all.

"Find your way," he said after a moment.

"If I'm the last Crescent Witch, what does that mean?"

"Aileen told me you might be the last thing standin' in the way of magic dyin' out for good."

I made a face. "That's not ominous at all."

"I'm sorry."

My gaze flew to his. "What for?"

"This wasn't how I imagined this going..."

Thinking about how I whipped his bare ass with the lamp cord, I snorted and then burst out into peals of laughter.

"What are you laughin' at?" he asked angrily.

"Whipping your ass," I replied, wiping at my tears.

"Ack, don't remind me." He rolled his eyes and playfully rubbed his ass cheeks. "It stung."

The mood had lightened significantly, but it wasn't long before I felt a tug of depression. Everything had been turned on its head, *again*, and I had no idea what to do. None at all. Who was Skye Williams? I felt like I should know, but I'd been so concerned with figuring out Aileen, I'd forgotten about who I was going to be in the wake of her death. Now, it had reverted to nothing but chaos. Fantastical chaos.

"I'm a witch," I said, my heart sinking. "Everything I've ever known is just...gone. Who am I? What am I supposed to do?"

Boone placed his hand on mine and tangled his fingers through my own. "I'm goin' to help you, Skye. We'll work out what to do together. You won't be alone in this, I promise."

We sat in the shade of the hawthorn for a long time, just existing. A shapeshifter and a witch.

Staring up at the hawthorn, I knew the Tower had finally been rebuilt.

CHAPTER 12

Needless to say, Buddy didn't make an appearance that night, though Boone made one the next morning.

Emerging out of the cottage, I lingered in the garden. The world seemed to have changed overnight. It was unseasonably warm, which was saying a lot since the Irish summer was as mild as a spring day back in Australia. I still needed to throw on a loose cardigan before leaving the cottage. Otherwise, I would catch a chill.

Meandering down the path, the flowers either side appeared more vibrant than usual, and the bees buzzing around the lavender were bigger and fatter than I remembered. I was still the same Skye who saw all these things yesterday, but the difference was...now I knew the truth. I was a witch.

As if knowing changed anything.

Boone was waiting for me outside Irish Moon. He was leaning against the wall chatting with Mairead, looking rather sexy in his skinny jeans, boots, and red and black checked shirt that was rolled up to his elbows. It was like his trademark uniform or something. A cross between farmer and hipster sheik.

"Skye," he said in his sexy Irish lit.

Mairead narrowed her eyes, clearly annoyed I'd interrupted her one-on-one time with her crush. If only she knew how foxy he really was.

"Hey," I said. "What's up?"

"Have you forgotten?" he asked, flashing me a wink. "You asked me to help you with some errands today. I've come to collect you."

I curled up my lip, not understanding what he was on about, and then I twigged. "Oh…" I declared, cottoning on to the fact he wanted to help me with my magic and was trying to spring me out of work. "Yeah, the *thing*."

"I guess I'm mindin' the shop on my own, *again*," Mairead complained.

"You love it," I retorted. "I'll give you a bonus."

"Fifty euro," the girl demanded.

"Twenty-five," I countered.

"Forty."

"Twenty-five."

"Thirty-five.

"*Twenty-five.*"

"Thirty."

"I'm not going a cent over twenty-five." I put my hands on my hips. "We can stand here all day if you like."

Boone was watching us with an amused expression, his head flicking back and forth like he was watching a tennis match.

Mairead stamped her foot. "Fine. Twenty-five."

"*Yes.*" I handed her the keys triumphantly.

"You owe me big-time," she said, turning to unlock the door.

"I owe you twenty-five euro!" I chortled as Boone and I began walking away. "See you later!"

"You two fight like sisters," he said as we moved out of earshot. "It's perplexin'."

"Mairead's cool. She reminds me of me when I was her age."

Boone tilted his head to the side. "A rebellious girl who dresses in head-to-toe black?" He looked me over and smiled. "Nah, I can't picture it."

"*Smooth*," I drawled as we wandered down the footpath while Mairead shot daggers into my back with her eyes. "So anyway, this is a surprise."

"It is?"

"After yesterday..." I trailed off.

"After yesterday, I'm surprised you want to come walkin' with me at all."

"Well, I don't think you're a pervert anymore if that's what you're getting at." I snorted, still unable to get the image of his bare ass out of my mind. It was a nice ass now that I thought about it.

"Lucky me."

"So how does it work?" I asked. "The whole...*you know*."

"It's instinctual," Boone replied, chuckling at my covert references to his shapeshifting.

"So that story you told me about Bully and Roy," I mused. "That had to do with the *thing*."

"Aye, I calmed him with me affinity. Only for a moment, though. Bulls are too wild to be tamed even by someone like me."

"And you can heal yourself?" I went on, as curious as a kid who couldn't stop poking a bug with a stick.

"To a certain degree."

"Like, what's the worst thing you've done to yourself that you've been able to fix?"

"You ask a lot of questions, you know that?"

"You're no fun," I said with a pout.

"I'm beginnin' to understand why Aileen was so annoyed with me," he muttered.

I waited a moment and then asked again. "Tell me. *Please?*"

He sighed, but I could see the hint of a smile pulling at his mouth. "Broken bones."

"No way! That's pretty impressive."

"You're takin' this really well," he said with a frown. "It's rather unexpected."

"I contemplated running away screaming yesterday, but it seemed excessive. Seeing you do your...*thing*? Well, I couldn't really claim ignorance after that."

He laughed as the hawthorn came into view. "I suppose not."

"You're cute as a fox."

"You think so?" He grinned, pleased with my declaration.

Standing under the hawthorn's branches, I glanced up, studying the dappled canopy overhead. So much had happened in this very spot, including the standoff with the wolf, but I wasn't afraid here. I felt an odd sense of calm as if a blanket had been flung over me and someone loving had tucked it in tightly. Boone was right when he said we were protected here. Now that I was beginning to understand the world I'd fallen into, I could feel it.

I wondered at the things Boone had told me about himself and how he'd ended up in Derrydun. Something had chased him here, and Aileen had found him. Before that, he didn't remember anything. I couldn't imagine it. Not knowing where I was born, who my parents were, or even my own name. Things must be tough for him, and no one had any idea. No wonder he'd been close with Aileen. She'd been the only one who'd known the truth.

"Does it bother you?" I asked, glancing at him as we approached the base of the hawthorn. "Not remembering who you were?"

"Sometimes," he replied. "In the beginnin', I struggled. I was like a newborn babe. I didn't know my name, what I looked like, or where I'd come from. I didn't even understand I was a shapeshifter. I was a fox first, then a gyrfalcon, and a man third. I asked so many questions that Aileen contemplated throwin' me out on me backside. She also saved me from myself a few times, so I mustn't have been too bad."

"She saved you?"

"Aye."

When it became clear he wasn't going to elaborate, I pressed him. "From what?"

"There are creatures out there that are tryin' to get home," he said reluctantly. "There used to be a hawthorn down in the gully behind Sean's farmhouse. I couldn't leave well enough alone even when Aileen warned me to leave it be. A creature was there, feedin' off the tree's magic, and it almost got me. Aileen said they were fae that had become twisted after they'd been cut off from magic. She called them craglorn."

"Craglorn." I tested the name on my tongue, and it sounded strange. "What does it mean?"

"The ravaged, *crag*, and the lonely, *lorn*."

"That's so sad. A thousand years is a long time," I mused. "I suppose they're starving."

Boone shrugged. "They would do anything to survive

and more still to get home. Don't pity them, Skye. They wouldn't hesitate if they found you. If it weren't for Aileen, I wouldn't be here right now."

Shivering, I wrapped my arms around myself, the rays of the sun filtering through the canopy doing nothing to warm me. Glancing around the clearing, the trees seemed to crawl closer, tightening around the hawthorn and us. Sucking in a deep breath, I began to feel exposed as the sounds of the forest amplified. Rustling, creaking, snaps, rattles, and birdcalls echoed through the thick woodland, and I turned, my skin tingling.

Craglorn...twisted, starving, magical creatures. It looked like the fair folk weren't so fair anymore.

"It sounds like someone's out there," I said, shivering as if we were being watched. "It's freaking me out."

Boone's lips quirked. "Nah. There's no one out there."

He held out his hand and beckoned me closer. Sliding my palm against his, he tugged me toward him.

"Listen," he murmured. "Hear that sound?"

"The fluttering and..." I listened. "The rustling."

"That's the leaves fallin' from the boughs overhead and findin' their way to the forest floor."

"And there's that cracking sound... It sounds like someone stepping on branches. Someone following us." I shivered, panicking slightly at the thought of other unseen people out here.

"Ah, that's old branches breakin' away from the trees and fallin' to the ground."

"How do you know?"

"I spend a lot of time walkin' out here."

"Why?" I frowned, wondering what the attraction was.

"It's quiet," he murmured. "I can think out here without

bein' distracted. And I can change if I want. I can run or fly without anyone seein'."

"You can fly?"

"Of course. It takes some time to create an affinity with a new animal, but I can change into several things."

"Like what?"

"A fox, a tabby cat, a gyrfalcon, and a horse. I'm sure I could change into Fergus's donkey if I tried, too."

"You can change into a horse?" I wondered what that would look like.

"I made friends with Mark Ashlyn's black stallion."

"Really?"

Glancing up, I realized how close we'd become and let out a little yelp. Tugging my hand from his, I wrapped my arms around my middle.

"I'm not much of a wilderness person," I said lamely. "The closest I got was my dad's house by the beach."

"The house by the bay?" Boone asked. "With the cargo ships that sailed in and out?"

My brow knitted, and I angled away from him. He sure seemed to know a lot about my life. Even more than me. Another wave of jealousy threatened to take control of my mouth, and my scowl deepened.

"You sure know a lot of fun facts about my life," I said irritably.

"Aileen used to talk a lot about you."

"Yeah?" I was much more open to talking about her after yesterday's revelations. If she were still here, then she would be able to tell me what to do, but she wasn't, which was why I was here in the first place. I would have to figure out this puzzle on my own with the limited expertise of a shapeshifter with amnesia.

He smiled, then nodded toward the tree. "Do you want to give it a try?"

"My magic?" I asked nervously.

"It's why we're here."

"I'm much more interested in talking about you," I said, trying to stall. "Is magic a universal thing? If you're a shapeshifter, does that mean you're meant to live over there? Is that where the witches came from? That other place?"

Boone chuckled and shook his head. "You're stallin', and no. I'm human at my core, and so are you. Magic lives in lots of creatures that aren't exclusively fae."

"Like Robert?"

"Aye, like Robert." He nodded at the tree again. "Now how about you give somethin' a try?"

I made a face and hunched over like I had an upset stomach. "How am I supposed to do that when I can't feel anything? Like, there's nothing in me that feels any different. Not before being zapped with Robert's magical pen or after. That sounds rather perverted when I say it like that."

Boone raised his eyebrows, his cheeks turning pink, and it was rather cute. He turned away and crossed the clearing. Squatting by the base of the hawthorn, he fossicked in the undergrowth before holding up a green leaf, the stem pinched between his forefinger and thumb.

"Do you know what you're doing?" I asked, watching him return with his find. "That's a leaf. What's that got to do with casting spells?"

"It's a hawthorn leaf," he retorted. "And I know a little. Robert gave me some pointers, but there's only so much I can do. The rest is up to you."

"Don't tell me there's some mystical prophecy about having to find my own path and learn my own lessons," I complained. "What a cliché."

Boone shrugged.

I threw my hands into the air. "Typical!"

"Concentrate," he coaxed, placing his hand on my shoulder. The movement was intimate, and I tensed as he held up the leaf in his open palm.

"What do I do? Make it float or something? How about bursting into flames?"

"How about floatin'? I left me fire extinguisher at home."

"Ha, ha. Real funny."

Narrowing my eyes, I had no idea what I was doing, but I tried to will the leaf to rise. Nothing happened. I screwed up my face and tried again, knowing I looked like I was borderline constipated. *This better not be one of those hidden camera shows*, I thought.

"Float, you little piece of—" Just as I was about to throw a tantrum, the leaf began to twitch in Boone's palm, and before I realized what was happening, it fluttered upward.

"Yes!" I fist pumped the air. "It worked!"

"Uh, it more than worked," Boone said, looking around the clearing.

Lifting my head, I gasped. We were surrounded by thousands of floating leaves. The effort I'd placed in making a single little thing float had blown out to a seven-meter radius. Wow, talk about putting your back into it.

Reaching out, I tapped a leaf, and it spun around once before settling back into place.

"How do they go down?" I asked.

"You're askin' me?"

"I don't see anyone else here." Sighing, I lifted my hands and held them out palm down. "Let's see... *Down!*" I waved my hands downward, and the leaves fluttered back to earth. I laughed. "Ha! Take that!"

"You showed them."

"Did I really do that?" I asked, twirling around. "It wasn't some illusion like one of those Las Vegas magician shows?"

"Aye. It was you," Boone replied, his voice echoing through the clearing. "Do you want to try again?"

"I..." I glanced around uncertainly, not sure I wanted to find out how deep this magic ran. Now that I'd disturbed it, I could sense something just below the surface of my skin. It tingled and crawled, unsettling my heart.

It was wonderful and amazing and all of those kinds of words, but it was also frightening. I was the last Crescent Witch. I was alone with a monumental task—protecting magic from extinction.

"Can we walk for a while?" I asked. "I just..."

Boone frowned but didn't press. "Sure. Of course, we can."

We walked for some time, venturing deeper into the woods than I'd ever been, but Boone seemed to know his way, so I allowed him to take the lead.

My thoughts rambled, and my uneasiness grew. I wondered what the tarot cards would say about this now that the Tower had played out. I made a mental note to draw a card when I got back to the cottage.

We must've walked a mile or so into the wilderness when Boone suddenly ground to a halt.

Turning, I asked, "What is it?"

"This is as far as I can go," he said mysteriously.

"What do you mean?" I screwed up my face.

"If I go any further, I step outside the protection of the hawthorns." He held up his hand like he was pressing his palm against an invisible wall.

"I don't understand. You're trapped in Derrydun?" It was absurd, but I'd seen stranger things.

"I told you somethin' was chasing me the night I came to

this place," he murmured. "If I step outside the boundary, they'll be able to sense me. I can't take the risk..."

I frowned, not liking the tinge of fear that had crept into his voice. It was pointless asking him who was after him because he didn't remember.

"Then we go back," I said, not making a big deal about it, but unfortunately, the weather did.

Turning my face toward the sky as the first drops of rain fell, I yelped. It was big, fat, and heavy rain, the kind that soaked a person through even though they were in a forest.

"Dammit," I cursed. I'd been so lost in my thoughts I hadn't noticed the weather turning.

Boone grabbed my hand and tugged be back in the direction of the hawthorn. "C'mon, I know a dry place."

We ran through the undergrowth, leaping over fallen logs, skidding across moss, and kicking aside ferns. My hair was dripping as the rain morphed into a full-on downpour.

"Here," Boone said, guiding me toward an opening that had appeared out of nowhere.

Making a break for it, I followed his lead, desperate to get out of the rain and someplace dry.

"It's a little cave," I said, moving inside. The scent of damp earth wafted up my nose, and the air around us closed in. "Wow."

"'Tis a druid's cave," Boone said, his voice sounding close in the heavy air.

I turned, my interest piqued. "Druids?"

"It's said they used to meet in caves similar to these to practice their faith in times of persecution. They were also safe havens in times of trouble or a dry place to rest one's head. They're mostly gone now, but you can still find some hidden in the forests."

It was a romantic notion, and the thought of the mystical

people made me think of Merlin and the Arthurian legends of Britain.

"Well, at least it's dry," I said, squeezing out my sopping hair.

He peered out of the opening. "We'll be here a while."

"What? Are you a weather whisperer now?" I asked, sitting on the dirt. I was soaked through, so no use worrying about a bit of dirt on my bum now.

"No, nothin' like that. I work outside a lot. I've come to know the rain. Ireland is famous for it, after all."

He sat next to me, and our arms touched, sending tingles all the way up and down my body. Shivering, I sank into my wet cardigan, and Boone, taking my movement to mean I was cold, wrapped his arm around my back.

He smelled like nothing I'd ever smelled before. All woodsy and spice. Nestling into his side, I turned toward him and studied the line of his jaw. He swallowed hard and angled his face toward mine. His eyes were so dark they almost looked black, but there were tiny flecks of chestnut through them. When he was a fox, they were a rich honey. He *was* cute as a fox, I hadn't lied about that, but as a man...*phwoar*.

"Skye..." he murmured, drawing attention to his mouth.

Realizing I was an inch away from kissing him, I turned away. Tucking my chin against my shoulder, my cheeks flushed scarlet. That was a really close call.

The last thing I needed right now was to fall in love with a shapeshifter. Everything was in chaos, and flinging myself into a romance with the one person who understood what I was becoming would only lead to more shenanigans I didn't have the heart to deal with.

At the thought of my heart, my mind turned to Aileen and her heart attack. The more I learned about this secret supernatural world, the more I was beginning to doubt. And that included the circumstances of her death.

"Boone?"

"Yeah?"

"If there are creatures out there hunting witches... Then... Was it really a heart attack that killed Aileen?" Now that the almost-kissed moment had passed, I was able to look at him again.

He hesitated, and I knew it had been a lie.

"Was it a craglorn?" I demanded. "Did it... Was she..."

"No," he said firmly. "No, it wasn't like that."

"Then what was it like?" He didn't move. He just sat there uncomfortably, not uttering a single world. "Tell me!"

"I... I went outside the boundary," he began, shifting away from me. "There was a woman who used to live here, though no one remembers her. Hannah. I thought she was like me, but she wasn't."

"What was she?" I asked as dread began to seep into my bones.

"She was one of the higher fae. A spriggan, she was. A spirit of the forest. *A trickster.*" He ran his hands over his face. "She broke my arms and legs and trapped me. It was Aileen who..."

He didn't have to say it. He'd been foolish enough to believe a fae, walked headfirst into danger, and my mother had to bail him out...*at the cost of her own life.*

"It was your fault?" I demanded, recoiling. "You were the reason she died?"

"Nay..." His expression was twisted in agony. "Nay, I wasn't."

"I trusted you!" My heart broke as I scrambled to my feet so fast I almost hit my head on the roof of the druid's cave.

"Nay, Skye, it was no one's fault. Let me explain..."

But I didn't want to hear anything he had to say. Bolting from the cave, I ran through the rain, leaping over logs, and sliding down embankments, trying to get as far away from him as I could.

"Skye!" he shouted after me. "Wait!"

His cries only spurred me on, my feet pounding on the earth as I fled back toward the village. I ran so far and fast I was back on the main road in no time.

Bursting into Irish Moon, the bell jingled furiously, and Mairead shot me a surprised look from behind the till.

"What happened to you?" she asked, curling her lip. "You're drippin' all over the floor, and I just swept there."

"I... I need a towel," I declared.

There was nothing else to say.

CHAPTER 13

I sat on the end of Aileen's bed, the spell book and tarot cards in front of me. Now completely dry, I was a sight warmer, but my heart was still a freezing block of ice.

A spriggan had killed Aileen? I didn't understand, which explained how I'd felt the entire time I'd been in Derrydun. I didn't understand the accent. I didn't understand my mother. Now I didn't understand the secret world of witches and fae that apparently coexisted with reality and mediocrity. Who knew what was real anymore, anyway? Not me.

Grabbing my phone, I tapped spriggan into a search engine. I could ask Boone, but I couldn't bring myself to look him in the eye. His stupidity had brought about my mother's death and everything that had happened to me since that day. He was the reason the Crescents had called me 'home.' He was the reason my life had fallen apart.

The Internet was no help with my spriggan search. All I found were silly stories about treelike creatures that apparently stole mortal babies only to replace them with changelings. And something about guarding buried treasure, which sounded like something from a video game. It also said they were ugly old men with big heads, which was a complete contradiction to Boone's story.

"What am I supposed to do now?" I asked the air.

She died saving Boone, and everyone thought she'd had a heart attack. How could he live with himself? Rubbing my tired eyes, I sighed. It was like she'd died all over again, only this time, I couldn't tell anyone about it.

Opening the tarot cards, I shuffled the deck, taking comfort in the repetitive motion. Taking a deep breath, I pulled a card from the middle of the pack, just to confuse the Universe, and turned it over. It was an image of a naked woman standing in a pond full of rushes. Above her was an array of stars, and she was holding a jug in either hand, filling them in the waves of twin waterfalls. She was called the Star.

Flipping open the book, I found the page describing her qualities. *The star hints at the possibility of rebirth. You have endured life's challenges brought forward by the collapse of the tower, and you are now open to healing and transformation if you choose to be open to it. The Star is a symbol of rejuvenation and hope. You may now be in a phase where you have to have faith in yourself and the world around you. A better future is possible, but you must remain steadfast.*

A better future? I snorted and tossed the card down. How was this a better future than the one I already had in Australia? Was being a witch supposed to be like this? Clueless and alone, hunted by twisted, starving creatures for my magic...magic I couldn't even feel inside me.

I'd made a bunch of leaves float, but that was at the hawthorn with Boone's help. Now that I was alone, the tingling sensation was gone, leaving me cold. I couldn't feel my power at all. Some Crescent Witch I was. Last in the line and they'd gotten a complete dud.

Shuffling the cards again, I drew another. There she was again. The Star. I put the card back and shuffled the deck a little more violently. I pulled another, but this time, from the bottom. The Star.

I drew again and again, each time turning the card over to find the same bloody thing. Every time, the Star. *Star, Star, Star.* I drew her so many times the word began to lose all meaning.

Letting out a frustrated cry, I flipped through the spell book, but the words ran into each other, making less and less sense as I went.

This was ridiculous. *I couldn't do it.*

"What am I supposed to do?" I exclaimed to the empty room around me. "I can't even light a candle. You know, like all those witches do in TV shows and stuff? There's the one with the witch and the vampires, and she's all like, *I found out I was a witch five minutes ago, and look at all these feathers just hovering in the air. I just need to raise my hands and poof!* Like she was some witch prodigy or something. I made a bunch of leaves hover, but I guess that had everything to do with the hawthorn and nothing to do with me. You know, I got a C minus is maths, but somehow, I don't think that counts. This witch stuff isn't like astrophysics, is it?" I waited for a moment, almost expecting a reply to my rant, but I only got silence. "C'mon, you don't have to tell me everything, I'm not a cheater, but just give me a little bitty clue. Please? An incy wincy clue? You know, incy wincy like the spider? Ah, *forget it.*"

My head started to throb like a headache was coming on, and I glanced around the room. What if the wolf came back? Boone had said someone had come looking after

Aileen's death like they were waiting to see if a Crescent Witch would show up and take over her duties. She'd left me in Australia with bound powers to protect me, and now I was exposed with no way to protect myself.

Oh, no. What if the wolf was a shapeshifter like Boone? What if it was hunting me for another reason? If I was right, and I couldn't get hold of my magic, then I would be up shit creek without a paddle. Anyway, if it weren't the wolf, it would be something else, and it would be all over red rover.

Aileen, why did you have to leave me? Springing off the bed in a fit of passion, I turned around and around, searching for something to grab. My gaze settled on the dresser, and I strode toward it, my heart beating frantically as desperation began to tear at my fragile emotions.

"Who were you?" I exclaimed, tearing through the drawers. "Tell me what I'm supposed to do!"

I pushed clothes aside, searching, hoping, desperate to find something, *anything*, that would give me a clear answer.

"You owe me this!" I said, fighting back a torrent of tears. "You left me all alone, and now you're doing it again! *I hate you!*"

Flinging open the closet, I pulled out clothes, tossing them over my shoulder and digging deeper. There were no hidden compartments or mythical door to Narnia, so I turned my attention to stomping on the floorboards. There had to be something here. I'd found the spell book, right? But...nothing else moved.

Bolting downstairs, I tore apart the living room, tossing books off the shelves and flipping through pages. I pulled the horrible floral cushions off the couch, but they were just ordinary pieces of furniture.

"You've got to be kidding me!" I shrieked. "Show yourself!"

In the kitchen, I opened cupboards, banged pots and pans, and leafed through recipe books but still found nothing out of the ordinary. There was nothing magical in this whole cottage.

Where would I find her? *Where...* I froze, my pulse racing.

Snatching my jacket from the kitchen chair, the house keys rattled in the pocket, and I raced outside, slamming the door behind me. Running through Derrydun, I saw the spire of St. Brigid's peeking over the treetops. Not giving one hoot, I rounded the end of the little church, skidded on the slippery grass, and fell to my knees beside Aileen's grave.

At some point, someone had placed some flowers beside her headstone, some red things I didn't know the name of, and the capstone had been set into place. It was a really nice grave if the dead gave a toss about what their remains were stuffed in after they'd crossed over.

Placing my hands on the stone, I closed my eyes and prayed. I had no idea if I was doing it right or if I was being reckless with something I would likely never understand, but I did it anyway. I needed my mother now more than ever.

I felt my mind fall through the earth, and dizziness almost brought me back, but I forged on. I sensed worms wriggling through tons of dirt and then a void. That had to be the coffin, but there was nothing. It was just a space filled with air.

The moment I realized the truth was the moment I felt a familiar presence behind me.

I didn't have to look up to know it was Boone. The one thing I could control was sensing his aura. His and no one else's. What was the definition of irony? Probably this.

"I can't feel anything," I said, not even glancing up.

"It's because she isn't there," he murmured, voicing what I already knew deep down.

Lifting my hands off the stone, I pushed to my feet and slid my ass onto the end of the empty grave. I didn't feel so bad about sitting on it now I knew no one was down there.

"I want to hate you," I whispered. "So much."

"I deserve it."

Allowing my head to fall into my hands, I covered my eyes and tried to halt my tears. For a woman I grew up despising, I sure felt drawn to her now.

"Tell me," I said. "Tell me how it happened. From the beginning."

Boone shifted from foot to foot before sitting beside me on the end of the grave. Above, the sun was beginning to set, the clouds broken enough for light to stream through. The sky was on fire, and every shade of red and orange streaked across the tops of the trees.

I shivered, burying into my jacket. The ground was still wet from the earlier downpour, and my jeans were soaked through at the knees. The mixture of old and new gravestones was as eerie as it was beautiful, made even more chilling knowing the story Boone was about to tell.

"Hannah used to be the bartender at Molly McCreedy's," he began uncertainly. "After...no one remembers her. Robert said it was because she was one of the higher fae. Trickery was her nature. She'd been livin' in Derrydun under our noses. For how long, I don't know. Well before I arrived, anyway. She said she'd been feedin' off the hawthorn behind Sean McKinnon's house."

"The hawthorn that died?"

"Aye." He nodded. "The one where I was attacked by the craglorn."

"How did she..." I swallowed hard.

"Hannah first appeared to me as a fox," he went on. "Though she didn't let on who she was until much later. Until she...changed in front of me. I thought she was a shapeshifter like me. I was so alone, Skye...to think there were others like me? It was worth the risk."

"You went outside the boundary," I stated. He'd already told me as much in his awkward, halting way.

"I had to know. It had been eatin' me up inside. The mystery of who I am. All the memories I have are of the last three years. There's nothin' else..." He sighed and began worrying the hem of his shirt. "At the time..."

"It was worth the risk?" I asked, my hackles rising. "Putting my mother in danger after all she did for you?"

"It was a trap," he said, grasping my hands in his. "Hannah led me outside the boundary and trapped me."

"What for?"

I narrowed my eyes, finally able to look him in the face. His hair had sprung back into tight ringleted curls from the rain, and his eyes were darker than usual. The regret and pain in them were as clear as day. *Good.*

"Someone is lookin' for me. For me, and now you," he said.

"Who?" I tore my hands away. "Stop beating around the bush, and just say it, Boone. I'm not messing around here."

"Hannah had made a deal," he went on, his cheeks paling, "with a witch named Carman. In exchange for me, she was guaranteed a chance..."

"A chance to what?" I demanded.

"A chance to go home."

"Home?" I snorted. "To the fae realm? I thought that was impossible!"

"Nothin's impossible with enough magic." He lowered

his head. "Aileen, she sensed the trouble I was in, and she came. She fought Hannah…"

"And Hannah killed her." It was a statement. Hannah, the spriggan, the trickster fae, had killed my mother.

Boone nodded. "Aileen took her down with her magic and Hannah… She dragged her…"

"*Don't say it.*" I covered my mouth with my hand and glanced away. The fae had buried her alive. That was why her coffin was empty. That was why she wasn't here.

"Skye… *I'm so sorry.*"

"Those stupid cards," I muttered under my breath. "That damned Star…"

"What?" Boone asked. "Did you draw somethin' else from the tarot cards?"

"The Star," I said sharply. "I drew the Star. No more Tower. Just Star, Star, Star, *Star…*"

"The Star comes after the Tower," he said, confirming what I'd read in the book. "In the months before… Aileen drew the Tower almost daily."

"What are you trying to say? Aileen was the Tower all this time?" My mouth fell open. "When you said 'out with the old, and in with the new,' it was true, wasn't it?"

"I think she knew somethin' was comin'," he said quietly. "But I don't think she knew it was goin' to be like it was."

I snorted and shook my head. "She never got to draw the Star."

"But *you* did."

"Screw the Star," I exclaimed in frustration. "It's all faith this and universe that. Well, screw the lot!"

"*Skye.*"

"I need to know what to do! I don't know what any of this stuff means, Boone. I can't… I can't see where I'm meant to step. *I can't feel my magic at all.*"

"Just give it some time," he said in an attempt to reassure me.

"We don't have any, and you know it. What if one of those crag-whatever's come looking, huh? What if the wolf comes back? I'm useless!"

"I'm here to help you," Boone said, wrapping his arm around me and tugging me against his side. "I made a vow to protect you, and that's what I'm goin' to do. No matter what. I owe my life to Aileen and the Crescents. I'm yours. Forever."

I'm yours. Forever. The words echoed around the empty cemetery and lodged into my heart like shards of broken glass. They dug deep, stirring something inside me I didn't want to acknowledge. Forgiveness, love... *Whatever.*

"*Boone...*" I moaned and fell against his side, unable to hold my tears back anymore.

Sobbing against his chest, I let it all out as he held onto me. The loss, the frustration, the fear of the unknown. I soaked his shirt through with my agony, and he let me. He kept his promise.

"We'll figure it out," he said soothingly. "We'll find your magic, Skye. It's in there. I've felt it." He tightened his grip and pressed his lips to the top of my head. "I won't let them touch you. I would die before I let them harm you."

CHAPTER 14

It was a weird feeling, having someone declare they would die for you. People said stupid things like that all the time, but you always knew when it came to the crunch, they would never go through with it. You know, the actual dying part. Most people were cowards, but not Boone. Boone meant every word.

Maybe it was my magic picking up on his intent, or maybe it was just the emotion he'd put behind his vow, but I believed him.

Something changed between us that day by Aileen's empty grave. Something I couldn't hold or visualize and something that didn't have a name. Whatever it was, I was happy it had shown up.

Shielding my eyes from the sun, I stared up at the tower house.

The other week, I'd learned the tree that was overtaking the outer walls was a rhododendron. The flowers were a vivid purple, only blooming for the first time in the past week, and the entire plant was covered with them, but Mary told me it was classified as a weed. It was an exotic species that had invaded foreign soil and was threatening to swallow Ireland's woodlands until there was nothing left. It was a stark comparison to my own plight and that of the magic that had once thrived here.

The rhododendrons were beautiful when they were in full bloom, but it was a smoke screen for the real problem. Much like the fae trapped on this side of the doorways, it didn't belong here.

Sitting in the meadow beside the ruins, I opened the spell book and began turning the pages. It felt safe here. The bubble surrounding Mary Byrne's tower house had a calming effect that settled my nerves and then some. Knowing the Crescents were related to her—she might've even been part of the coven—helped me forge a stronger link to my heritage

It was strange how things had settled the longer I'd remained in the village. I was becoming part of the furniture and found myself caring about the people who lived here. Maggie at Molly McCreedy's, Mairead and her pouty Goth ways, Mrs. Boyle and her broomstick, Fergus and his donkey-riding dog, and Mary Donnelly at the teahouse. Even Sean McKinnon and his drunken rants had become familiar parts of this strange place called Derrydun.

Now that I'd found out I was a Crescent Witch and my duty was to this place, things seemed to have fallen into place. Well, after I got over my shock at the circumstances. Now I just had to figure out how I was going to actually *be* a witch. There wasn't a manual for this stuff, but at least I'd found the spell book, which the Internet—the trusty Internet full of opinions and fake news—called a grimoire.

This particular book was the work of Crescents over hundreds of years—well, at least the bits they'd decided to write down—and it was the only remaining link I had to them. The pages were full of spells and invocations, instructions on how to create talismans, and even rituals to summon and invoke spirits and wild energies. The latter frightened the bejesus out of me, but I didn't mind the idea of creating a talisman for protection. With all the magic-starved creatures crawling around the wilds of Ireland, it seemed like a fantastic idea.

Taking out the little clear quartz necklace I'd bought from Irish Moon, I set it in my palm and studied the flaws in the stone, from the six sides of its natural growth in the earth, right down to its point. The flat end was dipped in silver and had a little ring set into the metal, and a silver chain had been threaded through the loop, which was long enough for me to put over my head without undoing the clasp. When worn, it settled between my breasts and was easily hidden underneath my clothes.

Apparently, quartz crystals were used for protection and capturing and changing bad energies. The intent of the stone matched the talisman I wanted to create, so all I needed to do was join the two together...or so said the spell book. This pendant was exactly what I needed for my experiment.

It was time to find my magic.

Setting the book onto the grass, I pressed it flat, anchoring the pages open with a rock. Reading over the incantation again, I held the quartz point in my palm and closed my fist around it. The chain was cool against my skin, but the crystal began to warm the longer I clutched it.

"I imbue this crystal with the power of protection. May it shield me in times of darkness. May it serve as the armor of the Crescent Witches." I took another breath and glanced around, but I was alone. "I imbue this crystal with the power of protection. May it shield me in times of darkness. May it serve as the armor of the Crescent Witches." Then, I spoke the words a third time to seal the spell, focusing my intent and searching for my magic.

I imagined a ball of golden light in my belly and willed it to grow, then I imagined it flowing into the little crystal. After a moment, I began to feel warm like I'd been sitting in the sun too long, and I wiped the back of my hand across my forehead, wishing I'd brought a bottle of water with me.

Lying back in the grass, I stared at the sky, clutching the crystal against my chest. Closing my eyes, the ball of golden light flared and then began to fade.

"Skye."

I moaned, swatting away a hand that was shaking my shoulder. "*Five more minutes, Dad.*"

"Skye. It's Boone. Wake up."

My eyes sprang open, and I saw Boone above me, his curly hair haloed by a brilliant blue sky.

"Boone?" I sat up with a start, almost head butting him.

"What are you doin'?" he demanded, throwing my equilibrium off-center.

"I was... I wanted to make a talisman," I muttered, feeling around the grass for the necklace. "For protection."

"You have to be careful," he said, scowling as I picked up the little crystal. "There are many—"

"Many things out there looking to suck me dry. I know," I said, rolling my eyes.

"Skye, you don't get it. This was reckless." He took the book from where it was sitting open on the grass and snapped it shut. "It's not a game."

"I know it's not!" I exclaimed.

"I was half a mile away, and I felt the pull of your magic," he said angrily. "I had to run all the way here. I thought somethin' had happened..."

"You have your clothes on," I said, my head still feeling like it was stuffed with cotton wool.

"I'm not a nudist, you know. I came here without changin'."

"Huh?" I rubbed the inner corners of my eyes, trying not to smear my mascara.

"Magic takes a toll," he said, sitting beside me. "You sent out a callin' card and then fell asleep because the spell was too much, too soon."

I gasped, not realizing I'd zapped my own energy to the point I'd conked out on the lawn. What if a busload of tourists had come along and started snapping Kodak moments? *How embarrassing.*

"You need to be careful with this." He wiggled the book under my nose. "Especially away from the hawthorn."

"The craglorn..." I said, my head dropping into my hands. "I just sent out a flare, didn't I?"

"Don't forget Carman," he reminded me. "There are more things than the craglorn to worry about. There's a bigger battle goin' on than either of us understands. We've been safe here with the hawthorn in the forest, but there will come a day when we're forced out from under its branches."

"I'm not sure I want to remember her at all," I complained. The mysterious witch who was supposed to be a thousand years old was searching for people like Boone and me. I didn't like the sound of a mystical battle for magic, either. Up until now, I'd been concerned with protecting Derrydun and myself, but Boone was hinting at something more sinister. Looked like this chapter of Skye William's awakening witch juju had a second installment coming out in theaters next summer.

"What else do you know about her?" I asked.

"All I know about her is three things." He counted each one off on his fingers. "Carman is an evil-hearted witch, who was banished from Ireland a thousand years ago. She's still alive after all this time. She's collectin' magic so she can reopen the doorways to the fae realm."

"Surely there are stories about her?" I asked. "Myths and legends? People have been writing about the fae for centuries."

"The problem with stories is they get twisted the more they're told," Boone said, picking at the grass. "Someone adds somethin', and someone else takes somethin' away. Before long, there isn't any truth left in the tale."

He had a point, which kind of explained my results with my spriggan search on Google.

"The doorways were closed around the same time she was thrown out," I mused. "Did she have something to do with it? She must have since she apparently wants to break back in."

Boone nodded. "It seems so."

"She's coming for me, isn't she? Like a destiny thing? The Crescent Witches were the most powerful coven in Ireland at their height, right?"

"Yeah, Aileen said they were, but we might get lucky." He didn't look convinced, and I began to regret my stupid meddling. "It may only be a craglorn who's noticed."

"*Great.*" I rolled my eyes. "That's still in the too hard basket."

"This isn't a joke," he scolded me.

"I know it's not! If one shows up, how do we kill it?"

Boone shrugged, which didn't ease my nerves. "Aileen used her magic. I was in my gyrfalcon shape, so I didn't see much. Just...golden light."

"Golden light. That's helpful." I snatched back the spell

book from his lap and shoved my head through the silver chain. The pendant settled against my skin, warming me. "There's got to be something in here." I licked my thumb and began swiping through the pages looking for references, wishing they'd known what an index was in the year whatever.

"*Skye...*"

"What?" I snapped. "I feel rotten, okay? I'm a stupid dumbass who knows sweet eff all! If a craglorn comes knocking, I have to make sure I can cut the bitch before it hurts anyone in the village. You don't know how to kill it, so I've got to find out for myself."

"Skye, you don't understand—"

"No! I don't! But I get I've made myself a target since you've just been lecturing me about it for the past ten minutes. This is my mistake to fix."

"Skye..."

"What?" I exclaimed, glaring at him. When he didn't answer, I said, "How else am I supposed to learn about my legacy? Huh? There's no one else around to teach me, so I've gotta take a stab at it. Do you know any other witches?" He shook his head. "And even if you did, could we trust them?"

"Unlikely," he muttered.

"Yeah, that's right. I'm not going to trust just any witch who comes along, so that means I'm in this on my own with a judgmental shapeshifter with amnesia. Give me a break, okay?"

Boone snorted and pushed to his feet. There I went digging myself into a hole and making all of this about me. I was such an insensitive jerk.

"Boone..." I tugged at the laces on his boots. "I'm sorry, I didn't mean..."

"If you're goin' to meddle with that thing, then at least go to the hawthorn," he said irritably.

I rose to my feet, clutching the book under my left arm. Grabbing the sleeve of his shirt with my right, I pulled him around.

"Boone, I'm sorry, okay? I messed up, and I didn't mean... It's not your fault you can't remember. You're not a witch or..."

"No, I'm not." His eyes were dark and cold.

"You're all I've got," I murmured. "Boone, I..."

My fingers loosened their grip, and I glanced down, grazing past his lips on the way. Feeling a blush creep into my cheeks, I let him go and hugged the spell book against my chest. This was one of those passionate after-fight kiss moments, but even after the almost kiss at the site of Aileen's empty resting place, I still shied away.

I guess I didn't want to overcomplicate things, but I knew it was an excuse so I didn't have to face his reaction. What if he rejected me? Boone was the only person who knew about me besides Robert, but I hadn't seen the lawyer since the funeral. I didn't want to count on another absentee figure.

Boone was all I had in this crazy world of magic. Boone the shapeshifter.

"Skye..."

My heart zinged as his hand cupped my cheek, his fingers tangling in my dark hair. Coaxing my chin upward, our gazes met.

The excited chattering of a group of tourists walking up the hill broke us apart, and I combed my fingers through my hair, straightening out the tangles. Boone jumped back about a mile like I'd zapped him with the static electricity I'd been carrying since Robert O'Keeffe electrocuted me with his golden pen. *Way to make a girl feel special.*

Glancing away, I shuffled nervously. "Lucky you found me when you did," I joked lamely. "Otherwise, I would have ended up as a meme."

"We're gonna disagree on things," he said. "But I won't leave you."

He guided me back toward the path and around the group of tourists who were pointing cameras and mobile phones up at the tower house in an attempt to add to their libraries of landscape photos.

"That makes me feel a lot better," I muttered sheepishly.

"Let me take you home."

"I don't want to go home."

"It would put me mind at ease until we know for certain nothin's creepin' about," he replied sternly.

"*Fine.*"

I allowed him to lead me back to the cottage like a naughty child, and to add insult to injury, I dragged my feet the entire way down the hill.

Boone deposited me on the stoop, waiting while I unlocked the door.

Turning, I couldn't quite meet his gaze. "I, uh..."

Reaching out, he brushed his fingers across my collarbone. Shying away slightly, I blushed when he tugged the pendant out of my top and rested it in his palm.

"Did it work?" he asked.

"I..." Plucking it from his grasp, I curled my hand around the quartz point and felt a hum vibrate through my skin. "I think so."

He smiled, the air still tense between us, or it just might've been my own embarrassment. After an awkward moment, he stepped down onto the path.

"Stay safe," he said, backing along the gravel between the lavender bushes. "I'll keep an eye out."

Tightening my grip on the quartz, I watched him disappear through the garden and around the corner onto the main road. *Why was I so stupid?*

Opening my palm, I frowned when I saw the clear crystal had taken on a lemony hue. Its core was tinged with a golden thread that only seemed to deepen the longer I stared at it. I guess the spell worked, after all.

Closing myself in the cottage, I hoped it was worth the hassle.

CHAPTER 15

Playing with the golden crystal hanging around my neck, I stared out the window of Irish Moon, mesmerized by another waxing crescent.

Outside, Boone was helping Mrs. Boyle weed her garden, his ass sticking up in the air. When I said Mrs. Boyle was helping, it was in the minimalist way possible. She was leaning against her weapon of choice—her broom— watching him do all the hard work. One eye was on the garden, the other was on the street, watching for children to chase.

Sometimes, I wondered why she lived in the center of town if she didn't like people that much. Only last week she clocked a poor schoolboy over the head with the end of her best straw broom. Then, when his mother came to waggle her finger at the old lady, she got a whack to match that of her son.

Mairead stood beside me and followed my gaze. Boone's ass was up in the air as he bent over to pull out a stubborn root, and for a guy who could morph into a tabby cat, it was pretty damn fine.

"Lovely view this mornin'," she declared, causing my mouth to fall open.

"Mairead!"

"So... Are you and Boone..." She raised her eyebrows.

"No," I shot back a little too quickly. "Boone and I are just friends."

Just friends, who've had too many almost-kiss moments and shared an outlandish secret no one would understand.

"Yeah, right," she said, rolling her eyes. "You need a bib you're droolin' so much."

"Don't tell me you saw him first because the age difference is phenomenal."

"Age has nothin' to do with it!"

"Age is a legality, Mairead."

She pouted. "Age of consent is seventeen, so there! Anyway, I'm eighteen in August."

"And you'll be in Dublin by then with a whole University full of hot men your own age."

"You're only sayin' that because you want him for yourself."

"I'm only saying it because it's true. You want to see the world, yeah?" She nodded. "If there's one thing I know about Boone it's that he's probably never going to leave Derrydun anytime soon. Do you want to be stuck here for the rest of your life for a pretty face?"

Mairead screwed her nose up. "I hate you."

"You love me," I declared, turning back to the window. "A crush is some harmless fun, but a relationship..." I sighed.

"What?" the girl asked behind me. "Have you had your heart broken by some Australian surfer guy?"

"Not everyone in Australia surfs," I said, rolling my eyes. "That's a cliché."

"*Whatever*. So? Did you?"

Looked like I wasn't going to get out of her cross-examination anytime soon. Turning away from the window and Boone's display outside, I rounded the counter and sat behind the till.

"Yeah," I said. "Right before I came here."

"What did he do?"

"He didn't do anything," I replied, taking out the tarot cards. "Sometimes, people grow apart."

"But you weren't expectin' it, right?"

"What's with the good cop, bad cop, Mairead?" I demanded, shuffling the cards.

I hadn't thought about Alex for over a month, and I wasn't sure if I should be relieved about it. We'd been serious, like weeks away from saying the L-word to one another kind of serious. Now that life felt like a dream, and it was already fading.

"Just tryin' to figure you out."

"There's nothing to get," I said, pulling a card from the deck. The Star. I felt better about this one and the having faith part now.

"So are you goin' to stay? After the summer, I mean."

I set the tarot cards down and sighed. I guess I was stuck here now that I knew I was a witch with a mystical sacred duty to the village. It wasn't so bad. Was it?

Thinking about yesterday's stupid episode at the tower house, I cringed. Nothing had shown up, but it had only been a day since Boone found me asleep in the meadow. There was still time to kill everyone with my stupidity.

"Yeah," I replied. "I guess I'm staying."

"So... Will you need some help in the holidays?"

Her face was lit up with such an innocent look of hope, despite the black lipstick she'd worn today. I nodded.

"Sure," I replied. "I guess."

There was no running from destiny.

It was a long day behind the counter at Irish Moon.

Three busloads of tourists shuffled around Derrydun and tramped through the store, buying up crystals, handmade wind chimes, books, and knickknacks, feeding the till. It was a fantastic day for takings, but my nerves were shot.

I didn't like looking over my shoulder for an enemy I wasn't even sure was coming.

By the time I made it back to the cottage, I was on edge. Thankfully, there had been no fae sightings among my customers, nor had there been any twisted and craggy monsters roaming about the main road, swinging from the branches of the hawthorn like a monkey.

I wasn't long inside when there was a knock at the front door. Tiptoeing down the hall, I peered through the stained glass but couldn't see anyone outside. Flipping the deadbolt, I opened the door a crack, but it was to fresh air. I was about to shut it again when a robust *meow* echoed through the air.

Glancing down, I saw Buddy sitting on the welcome mat, peering up at me with his big green eyes.

"Oh, it's you," I declared.

Buddy—aka Boone—meowed and sauntered inside, his body small enough to shimmy through the crack.

Closing the door, I saw him tear up the stairs in his cat form before a thump sounded overhead.

"You know, you don't have to show up as Buddy anymore," I called out. "Besides, you keep forgetting your clothes. People are going to start talking about your nakedness."

"If I kept showin' up as myself, they would definitely talk," he replied wryly, his voice muffled. "Mary keeps tryin' to send me off to the matchmakin' festival in Lisdoonvarna. Obviously, I can't go."

"What matchmaking festival?" I demanded, squashing down a pang of jealousy. Ugh, Mairead was so right.

"They have it in this tiny village in County Cork," he explained, coming back down the stairs, fully clothed. "It's a whole big thing. People from all over the world go hopin' to find someone."

"Where did those clothes come from?" I made a face. "Do you have a closet full of red and black checkered shirts or something?"

"Aye. Two weeks' worth, labeled with each day of the week."

"Really?"

"No, not really." He laughed and went into the kitchen.

"Good," I said, following him. "Because that would be weird."

"Weirder than bein' able to change into a cat?"

"Totally weirder."

"I left a few things here when I moved out," he explained, opening the fridge. "Where's all your food?"

"You mean, where's all the microwave meals?" I tapped the freezer. "Eat your heart out."

He flung open the freezer door, and his eyebrows rose when he saw the stockpile I'd amassed. I had roast chicken, beef, lamb, casserole, curry and rice, lasagna. Every food group was represented in a pre-cooked, snap-frozen form.

Boone shook his head, his curls falling into his eyes. "Ah, this is terrible."

"Hand me a frying pan, and I'll burn the house down," I said, puffing out my chest. "But hand me a microwave, and watch me surf the waves." I wiggled my hands like I was doing the hula, and Boone burst out into laughter.

Smiling, I pulled out a chicken dinner and opened the box, glad our fight yesterday seemed to be forgotten. At least until we knew we were out of the woods craglorn and crazy ancient witch-wise.

"You can't eat that nonsense," he said, taking the plastic tray out of my hands.

"Are you going out to get some real food?" I put my hands on my hips.

"Ack, not tonight," he commiserated, handing me back the frozen Frisbee. "I better make a selection."

"Try the beef. That one has a lot of vegetables in it."

Once we were armed with steaming plastic trays of food and decked out with cutlery and drinks, we set ourselves up in the lounge room among the cheesy floral furniture.

"You don't have to come over like this anymore," I said, stabbing a rubbery square of potato. "I'm fine."

"You know I can't let you out of me sight once it's dark. Not right now."

What he really meant was, *I can't let you out of my sight because your stupid talisman spell is probably going to get your soul sucked out by alien parasites.*

"Fair enough," I muttered, frowning when I saw he was staring at my boobs. "What are you looking at? My face is up here."

"The talisman," he said, causing my cheeks to flush crimson.

Glancing down, I saw the crystal had slipped out of my top and was sitting against the fabric of my dress...right over my boobs, which he wasn't staring at, *at all.*

"It was clear yesterday," he mused. "Now it's got a golden tinge."

"Is that to do with Crescent magic? You said Aileen…"

Boone nodded, raising his chin so he could gaze into my eyes. "You found your magic."

"Sure did." I rolled my eyes.

"It was a mistake, Skye," Boone murmured. "We all make them. I've made plenty."

I snorted and stabbed my fork at the little compartment of peas in front of me.

"Your talisman worked," he went on. "It's a clever thing to make."

"I can't be afraid to use my magic," I said. "I just need to hold back a little. I've been heavy-handed."

I expected Boone to start chastising me again, but he dropped his fork and raised his head, his eyes widening.

"What's up your ass?" I pouted.

"*Shh*," he hissed, holding up a finger.

Setting my own fork down, I listened to the silence outside. Before I arrived in Derrydun, I was so used to there being all kinds of noises. In the city, it had been the *whoosh* of cars on the street outside, doors slamming, neighbors playing music, dogs barking. At the beach, it had been the constant crashing of waves and the howling of the wind. Here, other than the rustling of leaves and the odd bird chirp, it was oddly quiet.

Whatever Boone was listening for, I couldn't hear it at all.

"There's nothing there…" I began, but he set his dinner aside and rose to his feet.

"It isn't close, but…"

"But what? Is it a craglorn?" I felt like puking.

"I'll be back," he said. "Stay here, and whatever you do, don't go outside."

"I'm so not going out there. But what about you? What if…"

"I'm goin' to change. Don't worry about me. This is me duty."

I didn't like the way he referred to us hanging out as some annoying task he was forced into doing, but I had no choice. I wouldn't admit it to his face, but I was afraid. Not just for me, but for him. I had no idea what a craglorn looked like in person, but the last time Boone went up against one, he was almost torn to shreds, and he was only able to escape with Aileen's help. What if it tried to attack him?

"Boone," I said, tugging on his arm.

"I'll be fine, Skye," he murmured. "I have to make sure…"

"Don't try anything stupid, okay?"

"I won't."

He smiled lopsidedly and smoothed my hair behind my ear. His touch was too intimate for my mixed emotions, but right now, I didn't give a stuff.

Reluctantly, I let him go, lingering in the lounge room as the front door opened and closed. My heart began to thrum, my skin prickling with goose bumps the moment I was alone.

I didn't hear him change, and I didn't hear him run or fly away. Neither had I heard the sound that had creeped him out, which wasn't doing much for my own nerves right now. Sharpened hearing must be one of the side effects of his shapeshifting. The silence must be deafening for him.

Peering through the curtains, I was expecting something to pop up from the garden bed underneath and exclaim, *rah!* But nothing stirred. Above, thousands of stars were shining like diamonds dusted across a piece of black velvet. It was an epic cliché, but I didn't have any other words to describe it.

Boone didn't come back for a long time. I ate the rest of my microwave roast chicken in silence, fretting for his safety, while his beef dinner went cold.

The moon dipped lower in the sky, the night darkened, and it was three hours before I heard him come back.

He padded into the lounge room, wearing nothing but his shirt and a pair of boxers, his jeans and boots in his hands. I didn't care that he was in his undies, I cared that he'd come back in one piece.

I jumped off the couch and flung my arms around his neck, squeezing him tightly.

"Oh, my God," I exclaimed. "I was beginning to think you'd been eaten."

"I'm all right," he said. "I flew over the forest, searchin'."

"Did you find anything?" I pulled back, my arms slackening around his neck, but I didn't let him go.

His expression was grave like he'd been sucking on a lemon, and my heart sank.

"It's lost," he murmured, dropping his jeans and boots.

"But it's out there." I let him go and fell back onto the couch. "I'm so stupid!" I fisted my hands in my hair and felt like pulling it out in clumps. "Why did I have to meddle in stupid shit I know nothing about? Why didn't I go to the hawthorn?" I let out a frustrated cry.

Boone sat next to me, not bothering to put on his jeans. Right now, I had more important things to worry about than his lack of trousers.

"It doesn't seem to know where to go," he said quietly. "It

was roaming around in circles, searchin'. It was a fair way from the village."

I made a face. "Still doesn't make me feel any better."

"It won't come out durin' the day, so we've got time to prepare."

"Oh, God," I said, flapping my hands around. *Deep fried shit on a stick.* We've got to kill it."

Boone nodded. "To be sure. We can't let it roam around here."

He was right. The only way to end this was to make sure the craglorn didn't reach Derrydun in the first place. We had to go out into the forest in the middle of the night and kill it.

"So..." I muttered, my heart heavy. "I have no idea what I'm doing, but I'll find a way to end it." *Or it would be the end of us.*

He slid his arm around my back and sighed. Everything was in that gesture, the burden I'd stupidly brought down onto my shoulders clear as the crystal hanging around my neck. Well, clear with a lemony hue.

I glanced at him, knowing I was the only one capable of putting the twisted fae down for good. The last Crescent Witch had to live up to her destiny. This was why I was called home, after all. The protector of Derrydun.

I guess it was time to add monster slayer to my resume.

CHAPTER 16

Peering through the crack in the curtains, I studied the dark garden outside.

Nothing stirred, but it didn't help settle my nerves. I knew the craglorn was out there, and I knew it was searching for me. Me, the idiot who called it here in the first place. The twisted monster starving for magic. *Moron.*

"We don't have to do this now," Boone said behind me as he dragged on his jeans and boots. "If it comes closer to the village, I can lead it away. I could confuse it for a few days to give us time to come up with a permanent solution."

"You know what they say about a festering wound?" I asked, turning around.

He made a face and shook his head.

"The longer you leave it to fester, the worse it'll get."

"That's a terrible punch line."

I raised my eyebrows. "Let me just think up something that includes puss and maggots, then." Now that he was decent and no longer parading around in his boxers, I sat back on the couch. "I need to deal with this now before someone gets hurt."

Boone didn't say anything. He just watched me stew in my own juices as my mind raced. How did I defeat something I'd never seen before with a power I'd hardly begun using?

"There's gotta be a spell or something in here." I opened the spell book—the grimoire—and began studying each page. Too bad some of them were written in languages that were similar to English but not. Went to show how words changed over the centuries. Unfortunately, ye olde English was not my forte.

"Aileen's magic was always instinctual," Boone said, seeming to have accepted my need for immediate action. "I never saw her chant or perform rituals."

"I can't rely on instinct," I complained, leafing through the spell book. "I need a backup plan."

"I've seen you cast spells, Skye."

"Yeah, little ones. All two of them."

"That packed a punch."

"What if I choke?" I asked. "What if I freeze just as the craglorn tries to suck me dry? What then?" I raised my eyebrows. "I would be a wrinkled prune." I made a slurping sound, then smacked my lips. "Bam. Dehydrated."

"I don't think it works that way," Boone said, making a face.

"I don't really want to find out. Anyway, I can't just hold up my hand, shape it like a pretend gun, and go *pew pew!* I'm pretty sure I would be insulting the entire Crescent bloodline by pretending I'm an extra in *Star Wars*."

He snorted, and my head shot up. He was stifling a laugh, which wasn't helping my mood.

"Boone!"

"Hey, you said it." He held up his hands in mock surrender. "What do you need me to do?"

"Be quiet. That would be a good start."

Focusing on the challenge ahead, I turned the pages of the spell book, allowing my thoughts to mull. The fae had been trapped here a thousand years, so there had to be a clue in there somewhere, right? The Crescents were epic badasses who'd have to have faced off with them before. This book was the coven's answer for a Bible. There had to be an origin story in here somewhere. I was just missing it in my naivety.

I wished there was a page labeled *craglorn one-oh-one*. It would make my life a lot easier, but I knew this was one of those 'life lesson' moments. If I got through this, I was so making a cute graphic with an inspirational quote slapped on it. Hashtag adulting.

Glancing at the clock on the mantle, I saw it was one a.m. Boone was slouched on the couch beside me and hadn't once complained. His eyelids were drooping, so he was either trying not to drift off or he was a total weirdo who slept with his eyes open.

"Stop lookin' at me like that," he mumbled.

"Like what?" I smiled sweetly.

He rubbed his eyes and sat up.

"Okay, I think I've got this down." I took a deep breath. "I can create a magical net to trap the craglorn, but I need a place to anchor it to. Since I'm essentially a newbie, I should probably use the hawthorn in the forest. It's powerful, can help me control my magic, and will act as a lure. Then we just need a way to finish off Mr. Craggy for good."

"Mr. Craggy?"

"*Mr. Craggy.*" I thought for a moment. "How do you kill a fae? I mean, can we just cut off its head?"

"You want to decapitate a craglorn?" Boone's eyebrows shot up.

"Yeah?" I began to feel uncertain.

Boone opened his mouth and shut it again, looking uncomfortable. He wanted to say something but was too pussy to say it.

"Spit it out," I demanded.

"Aileen... She used magic and only magic."

"You think the only way to kill it for good is to use magic?" I snorted. "Stands to reason." I opened the book again.

"You might be able to hurt it but not mortally."

"Then we make a magical dagger!" I turned around the page I'd found and showed him. Some long-dead ancestor had drawn up schematics for a weapon to protect against the fae, and it sat before me, the thick book of spells finally revealing something I had a shot at understanding. Besides, this witch's handwriting was completely A-plus material. I'd give her a gold star.

"A dagger?" Boone peered at the book, clearly not understanding. His shapeshifting juju was instinctual, and I suspected it was linked to his emotions more than anything, so recipes and maths equations were likely beyond him. In a magical sense, not a flunk out of year seven maths scenario.

"There's a way to charge a dagger with the power required." I pointed to the page, running my fingertip over the words. "*Saeclum naeniam.* Is that Latin?"

"Yes, I think so."

Tracing the lines of the pentagram inked onto the page, I wondered who'd written it. Whoever it was, thank goodness they'd chosen to immortalize their spell.

Picking up my mobile phone, I opened a web browser and copied in the words I couldn't make out.

"*Saeclum naeniam,* a spell for the *subiit deserta,*" I said, then read off the clumsy translation that had appeared on

Google Translate. "Dissolve incantation, a spell for the forlorn. This has to be it! You called them the ravaged and the lonely."

"Yeah, but..."

"But what?"

"Are you sure you can handle all these spells?" Boone asked with a frown.

"I have to. There isn't any other way around it unless you have an idea. The floor is open. Take the mic if you want." He shrugged, so I went back to plotting world domination. "*Aqua fons*... Spring water... *Cruach Phádraig*... Is that last part Irish? This is confusing."

"*Cruach Phádraig*," Boone said, correcting my messy pronunciation. "Croagh Patrick."

"What's that?"

"Croagh Patrick is a mountain to the west of here," he explained. "The peak of St. Patrick. It's a holy site."

"Then there's a spring at the mountain that can charge the dagger," I said excitedly. "If it's a holy site, then it must be the key to the spell..." My expression faded as I saw the look of fear that tinged the corners of Boone's mouth. "The boundary..."

"I can't go."

"Then I'll go alone."

"Nay, Skye..."

"No biggie," I said when in reality, I needed an adult diaper. "It's a test, is all. This is my first outing as a Crescent Witch. We'll figure the Croagh Patrick part out later. Now we need a dagger." Where the hell was I going to find one of those? There wasn't time to order from eBay. "Wait, I found the book under the floorboards. Maybe there are more hidden compartments. Give me a hand."

I began scrambling across the floor, bashing my fist. I

knew it was fruitless because I'd tried the same thing the other week when Boone had told me the truth about Aileen. I'd ripped the cottage apart and found nothing.

"I don't think there's anythin' there," he said, watching me crawl around the floor with my ass in the air.

"You lived here," I complained. "You never saw Aileen with a dagger?"

"The most I ever saw was a steak knife. I doubt she left a dagger layin' about the cottage. I never saw her with any ritual objects."

"So no cauldrons?" I pouted.

"No broomsticks, either."

"Hang on..." An idea began to form in my mind. "Does it have to be a dagger? Or can we improvise?"

Boone shook his head, clearly not a fan of where I was going with my lightbulb moment. "I don't think it's a good idea to try to stab a craglorn with a butter knife."

"Duh, of course, not. There's a big knife block in the kitchen. Lots of pointy things good for hacking."

"You're startin' to scare me."

"Says the naked Irishman." I rolled my eyes.

"I'm never goin' to live that down, am I?"

"Nope, and I'm going to take great pleasure in reminding you."

Turning back to the book, I thought about the logistics of using a carving knife. Was stainless steel hardy enough to store enough magical energy from the spring at Croagh Patrick to defeat the craglorn? Ugh, it probably had to be silver or something even rarer. Knowing my luck, it would have to be made from the metal from a comet and dusted with particles from its icy tail during the smithing process. It would have to have a flawless ruby set into the hilt that had to first be swallowed whole by a pregnant deer, roasted in its stomach acid, then shat out on a full moon. Where was I going to get something like that on a day's notice?

Then it hit me like a ton of bricks. The feeling of certainty that smacked me in the face was so strong I almost puked out of both ends in excitement. This must be the intuition thing Boone was telling me about.

"The tower house," I declared. "It feels weird up there. Like it's in a bubble... That's why I went to the meadow to cast the talisman spell in the first place. I felt protected there." I leaped to my feet. "Mary Byrne was a Crescent Witch!"

Boone stood. "You think somethin' is buried up there?"

"You said to follow my intuition, and it's telling me the answer is there." I shivered, shaking out my arms and legs and blowing a raspberry. "I'm all tingly."

"The ruined tower house?" He didn't seem convinced, but it didn't matter. I was sold.

"I'm going to need a shovel!" I declared. "Post haste!"

Wandering outside in the dark had never worried me. Not until tonight.

We found a shovel in Aileen's garden shed. Boone changed into a gyrfalcon—while my back was turned, and my fingers were in my ears—and now we were making a silent dash toward the tower house on the hill.

The moment we hit the small arm of woodland that separated the back of the cottage from the hill, Boone settled on my shoulder, wanting to be near until we reached the tower house.

It was the first time I'd seen him in his falcon shape, and he was rather handsome. His feathers were all white with dark speckles, his beak was hooked and razor sharp, and his eyes were golden and bright. His talons were poking painfully into my flesh but not hard enough he broke the skin.

I snorted, causing him to swivel his head toward me. This was totally weird. A man, who was a bird, was sitting on the shoulder of a witch as they climbed a hill, armed with a shovel so they could look for buried treasure. I was living in a strange reality—that was for sure.

When we broke through the tree line and stepped out into the open, Boone leaped off my shoulder and wheeled overhead, securing the perimeter.

Staring up at the outline of the ruins against the star-studded sky, I stepped forward, sensing the same strange bubble of protection that had drawn me here in the first place. It was Crescent magic that had marked this place, so was that why I could feel it so strongly? Made sense.

Standing in front of the iron door that separated me from the interior, I picked up the rusty padlock and shook it. It didn't budge, which came with zero surprises, so I dropped it and peered into the darkness. My gut was telling me to go inside the scary dark ruins. Hopefully, it wasn't the same as when people ran up the stairs in horror movies. Always a bad move.

Taking a deep breath, I blew it out and cracked my knuckles. Just a little bit of magic to bust the lock. No biggie. Light as a feather.

"Doorus unlockyus," I whispered, blurting the first thing that came to mind. *Doorus unlockyus?* I'd said stupider things in my lifetime.

The lock popped open, and I fist pumped the air in triumph. *Bam! Who was stupid now?*

Tossing the rusted padlock aside, I opened the gate, the

hinges squeaking loudly in the silence. Wincing, I turned and scanned the hillside, but nothing stirred. Overhead, Boone chirped softly, giving me the all clear.

The first room was pitch black. Stepping through the darkness, the scent of damp earth filtered up my nose as I felt my way with my free hand out in front and the shovel tucked under the other. I bashed into a wall and cried out, rubbing my nose. Feeling along the stone, I found an opening, my gut guiding me through.

Then I was outside again. The roof of this room had caved in at some point, leaving rubble strewn on the ground. I picked my way over it, glad for some moonlight to guide me instead of my clumsy fumbling.

Above, a shadow flicked through my peripheral vision, and I yelped, but it turned out to be Boone settling on the wall overhead. He ruffled his feathers and moved from foot to foot, finding a comfortable position where he could watch the hillside and me at the same time.

"Have you ever seen the movie *Predator*?" I asked.

Gyrfalcon Boone tilted his head to the side.

"It's about these commandos in the Amazon jungle who end up being hunted by an extraterrestrial warrior," I went on. "I feel like we're in that movie. You know, without the tropical jungle part. And without the automatic submachine guns and rocket launchers and commando training." That craglorn had better not be a Predator.

Turning around, I surveyed the room. There was no telling what it was used for back when the tower house was intact. All that was left was moss and lichen encrusted limestone. Any wood or furnishings had been removed or rotted away long ago. Through the crumbled roof, I could see the rhododendron towering toward the sky, its branches invading and pushing the walls apart. One day, there would be nothing left of this place but a pile of rocks overgrown by nature.

Focusing on the far corner, I lifted the shovel and speared it into the damp earth. I hardly made a dent. Stomping my boot on the end, I worked it deeper and began digging, hoping I would find the buried treasure before the sun rose. Seriously, I could be the pirate, and Boone could be the parrot on my shoulder. *Shiver me timbers!*

I was just getting into a rhythm when the tip of the shovel hit something hard. Hoping it wasn't a rock, I scraped back the dirt, and my heart leaped when I saw it was some kind of metal. Working the shovel around the edges, I coaxed it out of the earth, and when it was loose enough, I tossed the shovel, fell to my knees beside the hole, and dug it out with my bare hands.

Finally, prying it free, I held the metal box in my hands. It was a little longer than my forearm, narrow and made out of iron or tin—I couldn't tell which. It was the perfect size to hold a dagger. Scraping the dirt off the top, I wrestled with the latch.

"Do I need to do the doorus unlockyus thing again?" I threatened the box. "*I'm a Crescent, you know.*"

The latch sprang open as if I'd scared it into submission, and I opened the lid. Inside sat a thin, silver dagger, its hilt decorated with gold and silver Celtic knotwork. It looked like it should be on display at a museum someplace, sitting on a pedestal with fancy lights shining on it, complete with a little plaque.

"Oh, yeah," I declared. "*Pay dirt.*"

Lifting it out of the box, I turned it over in my hands, surprised at how heavy it was. It looked like a mini sword but was only the length of my forearm from hilt to tip. Inspecting the design, my gut feeling was further solidified when I picked out the golden crescent moons among the silver lines and swirls.

I glanced up at Boone and grinned. "Told you so, and we didn't even have to get a pregnant deer to shit at midnight under a full moon."

Now all I had to do was get to Croagh Patrick and find the spring...without Boone. It sounded easy as pie, but like him, there was no telling what awaited me outside the influence of the hawthorns.

Too bad, so sad. There was no other way.

CHAPTER 17

It turned out the dagger's correct name was an athame. And the spring at Croagh Patrick? It was the lifeblood of Ireland. The waters that fed the land from the belly of the earth itself. Or so said the spell book.

The ghosts of my ancestors had led me to the tower house the night before, and the next morning, I hoped they would lead me to the spring. Boone couldn't leave the protection of the hawthorns, so I had to go it alone. A stranger on strange soil with nothing but Google Maps to guide me.

We'd parted ways before the sun came up, and I'd dozed on the couch before the alarm on my phone practically slapped me awake. The plan was for me to borrow Sean McKinnon's car, with Boone vouching for my exemplary driving skills, and drive the two hours to County Mayo where I would begin my search at the foot of the mountain. I had a few clues in the spell book and an Internet search as to the location of the spring, but I wouldn't know for sure until I got there.

Boone was adamant the craglorn wouldn't come out until it was fully dark, so I had time.

Dressing in a comfy pair of black jeans, a plain gray short-sleeved T-shirt, and my trusty combat boots jammed onto my feet, I packed my few essentials—mainly the athame and my phone—into a bag that slung across my chest and went to Irish Moon.

Mairead was waiting for me out front, lingering in a spot of shade under the eave. She was dressed in a cute black dress with tiny purple flowers printed on the fabric, big black boots, and her hair in twin French braids. She had mad style, that kid.

"Hey," she said when she saw me.

"Mairead…" I smiled sweetly, dangling the keys in the air. "Mairead old buddy, old pal."

She scowled. "You've got dirt on your face."

"Are you able to spot me today?" I wiped the back of my hand over my cheek.

"Again?" she exclaimed, knowing exactly what I was going to ask before the words left my mouth.

"I'll give you a bonus. A better one this time and a kickass reference."

"You better." She pouted and snatched the keys from me.

"Consider this a promotion to assistant manager. I couldn't do this without you."

Her eyes lit up, but she instantly shook it away and pretended to be aloof about it. "You better. You've taken more days off than you've been here."

"Have not!"

"Feels like it." She pouted and turned to unlock the door.

Behind us, the squeal of tires drew our attention as a car screeched to a halt. We both turned to find a little red

Toyota Corolla idling with Boone behind the wheel. This must be Sean McKinnon's car.

"You're skippin' out to go on a date with Boone?" Mairead exclaimed.

"No! I'm borrowing Sean's car, and Boone said he would bring it by so I didn't have to walk all the way over to Roy's."

"A likely story," she said, pushing into Irish Moon, leaving me standing on the footpath.

Rolling my eyes, I turned to the car. Her crush wasn't working out so well, and knowing how messed up I'd been at that age, I felt a pang of sympathy. Being seventeen was a pain in the ass. It was old enough you had the urge to forge out into the world on your own but still too young to be able to do it legally and with your parents' permission. I'd been exactly the same as her, maybe even worse.

The car window rolled down, and Boone's head appeared.

"Jump in," he said, leaning across the passenger seat.

"You're coming? Mairead's already pissed off at me."

"Why?"

"Ugh." I rolled my eyes. "Why do I bother?"

Boone raised his eyebrows and flipped the lock. "Jump in before I change me mind."

"But what about...*the thing.*" I glanced around the empty street, looking extremely shifty.

"Like I said, I have to leave *the thing* sooner or later. I can't keep stickin' me head under the sand and hopin' whatever out there will go away. This is important. We'll work better together."

I made a face and opened the car door, sliding inside. "I hope you know what you're getting us into."

"So do I." He checked the mirrors and planted his foot

on the accelerator, careening around the hawthorn and tearing through the traffic lights.

"On second thought," I declared, holding on for dear life. "I hope I know what I'm getting *myself* into."

Nothing happened when Boone left the boundary. At least, nothing noticeable, so for now, it seemed like we'd gone undetected.

We spent the two-hour drive talking about stupid things like had Boone seen *Game of Thrones* and if he was team Lannister or Stark or even if he was team Targaryen. We talked about what our favorite colors were—his was red, which explained the shirts—coffee versus tea, Guinness versus cider, was there an Ikea in Ireland so I could change the floral furniture in the cottage, and the completely outlandish topic of 'what animal do you want to change into next.' The answer to that one was definitely a tiger and definitely not a flamingo.

By the time we saw Croagh Patrick, it was creeping closer to midday. The peak itself rose high into the sky, its tip green and gray, the snow having melted months ago. The fields below were a startling emerald color, trees and sheep dotted the landscape, and a town glittered in the distance. I was beginning to understand why the tourists who passed through Derrydun always had their cameras in their hands. Ireland was breathtakingly beautiful.

Parking the car in a spot furthest away from the entrance to the Visitor's Center, Boone killed the engine and glanced at me.

"You drive like a crazy person," I said, unclipping my seat belt.

"I'm not used to it."

"I'll say. Do you even have a license? How did you get one without any ID? You totally had a fake one made, didn't you?" My mouth dropped open.

"I don't have a license," he said, scratching his head.

"No!" I gasped dramatically. "And I let you drive!"

Getting out of the car, we stood in the sunshine, staring up at the mountain. It wasn't a big monster of a thing, not compared to the Himalayas or the Rockies, but it was big enough. Even from this distance, we could see the shapes of people walking to the summit. My thighs were already burning just looking at it.

"Where do we start?" I asked, shielding my eyes from the sun. "Should we ask at the Visitor's Centre?"

"They would know the area. This is the furthest I've ever been...that I can remember."

He was looking uncomfortable as if the world was giving him a severe case of shell shock, so I took his hand and led him toward the chaos.

The Visitor's Centre was teeming with tourists, who were arranging a variety of activities. Horse riding down on the beach, leisurely hikes, bike riding, and pilgrimages to the summit where a chapel dedicated to St. Patrick stood. The smell of freshly roasted coffee wafted from the cafe, and the air was filled with the murmuring of people shopping for souvenirs at the gift shop.

A lady behind the information desk armed us with a map detailing the various walking trails, pointing out locations of ponds and lakes, not knowing if there were any underground springs in the area. She explained that all the water in the catchments came from the melt.

Outside, we studied the map, comparing it to the satellite image on my phone.

"There's gotta be some kind of underground water source," I said, feeling lost. "The book said the athame must be charged with the lifeblood of Ireland. The water from the spring is the only way."

"It may have been hidden with magic," Boone offered. "Maybe that's why no one knows."

"Great," I declared, glancing up at the sky. "Thanks, Universe. Thanks, a lot."

We set out, climbing the track toward the summit. When we reached the first marker, I stopped and glanced back down into the valley. It was a beautiful view of the rolling hills, the farmland, and we could even see the ocean and the beaches that wrapped around the coastline.

"Look at this," Boone said, waving me over. He was standing by a slab of rock that was pockmarked with different sized holes and a few spiral designs.

"The map says it's called the Boheh Stone or St. Patrick's chair," I said. "It's Neolithic rock art. The dots are meant to represent the stars of the Milky Way."

Boone peered at it, looking unimpressed. "If you say so."

Ignoring him, I knelt down by the slab and pressed my palms against it. The dark surface was spotted with gray and yellow lichen, much like everything else around us. The swirls and holes people had carved thousands of years ago were still prominent, though I could see time and weather had worn out the edges. To think I was touching the same rock as ancient people had. Mind. *Blown.*

Someone cared enough about this place that they wanted to carve a specific design into the rock here. I wondered what it was for.

"I can feel something," I said. "Though I'm not sure if it's a magic thing or just my bowel movements."

"There's a bush over there."

"Real funny." I rolled my eyes. "But I think we're close. Something feels... It feels like it's rushing past me."

"Let's have a look around. It's likely off the path someplace. The rock is a good sign."

"Do witches have a link to the earth?" I asked as we ventured off the track and made our way down the slope.

"Maybe. I don't really know."

"When I focus, I can kinda feel things. Like back there at the rock."

"I suppose it's possible," he replied as we searched. "The Crescents are linked to the hawthorns."

Liking the idea I could talk to nature, we fanned out in our hunt for the spring. There were a lot of outcroppings of rock, lonely windswept trees, and grassy knolls but no sign of water. The day was dragging on, and we still hadn't found a single thing. Maybe after all this time, all the water had dried up.

"Here!" Boone cried, appearing from behind a rock.

Scrambling down the incline, I rounded the boulder and saw nothing but a wall of gray limestone splattered with yellow lichens.

"It's a rock," I drawled.

"It's a *pretend* rock." He waved his hand through the stone, and my eyes widened.

"*Cool...* Let's go inside." I stepped forward, but Boone held me back.

"I'll go first. We don't know what's in there."

"Stop trying to freak me out. Just because I'm a woman, doesn't mean—"

"Don't complain, Skye. 'Tis nothin' to do with bein' a woman." He took a deep breath and stepped through the rock, disappearing from view.

My skin tingled, and I glanced over my shoulder, but we

were still alone on the side of the mountain. Below, the world was spread out, looking more like a painting than actual reality.

"I can hear water," Boone called out, his voice echoing out of the rock. "There's a cave back here."

"Can I come inside?"

"Aye. Come in."

I stared at the rock with an uncertain feeling in my gut. I knew it wasn't real, but it looked like it. I just had to step through and... Lifting my hand, I poked the rock, and the tip of my finger disappeared through the surface. I was touching air, but my mind was freaking out, not able to join the two realities together.

"Close your eyes and walk through," Boone said. "I'll catch you."

I snorted and shook my head. Ignoring him, I waved my hand through the rock, and feeling bolder, I stepped through into the mouth of a cave. The air was cool, the earthy scent reminding me of the druid's cave back in Derrydun, and in the distance, I could hear the trickling of water.

Glancing over my shoulder, I scowled. The illusion was one sided, so in here, I could see right out, and my cheeks flushed. Boone must have had a good laugh at my fumbling.

"C'mon," he said. "Let's find the spring, and see if this works."

Delving into the darkness, I held up my phone, using the torch app to light our way. Shadows lengthened as we stepped carefully, descending into the earth. The further we went, the colder it became, but finally, the passage expanded until we stood in a little cavern. One end was made up of fallen boulders, and through the cracks, we could see the sky peeking through, but the ancient cave-in wasn't what panicked me the most. It was the mass of shadows that wriggled around a large pool of water.

That was definitely the spring, but I had no idea what those things were. They looked like inky black worms in the midst of a feeding frenzy.

"Ugh," I declared. "What are they?"

"Sluagh," Boone said.

"Sluagh? It sounds like you're hocking a loogie."

He glanced around the rock, looking for something while keeping well away from the edge of the little pool.

"Boone, what are they exactly?"

"They're shadow fae," he explained. "They're known for snatchin' souls."

"That's not ominous at all." I scowled at the shadows, who seemed more interested in hanging around the spring than they were in us. "We've got to get them out of the way."

"Any ideas?" Boone was as mystified as I was.

"Poke them with a stick."

"I'm not pokin' them with a stick," he grumbled.

"We need to distract them so I can get in there. What do they like to eat other than souls?" I asked.

"I don't know everythin', you know."

"Can you change into something, and lure them away? Just for a moment?"

"No, they'll swarm me." He glanced at me and then looked around the cave. "I've got an idea. They want magic, so we need to give them some."

"You want me to cast a spell?" I wasn't sure how I was meant to do that when I didn't know any spells and had been told to not be so frivolous away from the hawthorns.

"Aye. Unless you have another idea."

Glancing at the sluagh, I narrowed my eyes. They were a

disgusting sight with their wobbly human forms, neither solid nor transparent. If that were a thing. They were all face first in the spring, their legs flailing in the air, and if things weren't so dire—and they didn't eat souls—I would've made a dirty joke.

"Okay..." I murmured, racking my brain. "What do shadowy inky fairies like more than fresh spring water?" Picking up a palm-sized pebble, I held it up toward the light. "How about a game of fetch?"

Boone tilted his head to the side, clearly confused. Focusing on my magic, which was still an unknown—I wasn't sure what I was reaching for, or what it felt like—I closed my fist around the rock and willed it to do what I wanted it to do.

"Hey, you!" I cried, my voice echoing around the cave. "Sluagh off!"

I pulled my arm back and propelled the rock forward, throwing it toward the opposite end of the cavern. The pebble bounced against the rock fall, clattering and making an awful racket. The sluagh stopped their wriggling at the spring, and in a whoosh of air, the shadows flew across the cave, chasing my magical tennis ball like a pack of chocolate Labradors.

"Holy guacamole!" I declared.

"Quick, the athame."

I slipped the strap over my head and set my bag on the rock. Taking out the checkered tea towel I'd put the athame in that morning, I unwrapped it. Holding the dagger by the hilt, I plunged the entire thing into the water and hoped for the best.

At first, nothing happened other than my hand almost dropping off the water was so cold, but then a dull glow started to permeate the spring.

"Something's happening," I said excitedly. "You see that?"

"Aye," Boone replied, one eye still on the sluagh. "It's workin'."

I sighed in relief as the light began to grow, revealing strange markings on the dagger. From hilt to tip, it writhed with a growing power. Deep down, I knew this was what we needed to defeat the craglorn. It had to be.

"There," I said, pulling the athame out of the water. "Glowy symbols on a magical dagger. That's a good sign." I set it back onto the tea towel and wrapped it up, shoving it safely back into my bag. "Let's get out of here."

The second the words left my mouth, the sluagh rushed toward the spring, tearing past me in a torrent I couldn't fight. My feet slipped on the rock, and I fell. I cried out, reaching for Boone's hand, but I was swept under the water.

I lost all control, my bones chilling as I was completely submerged in the spring. Holding my breath, I fought against the shadows, alarmed at the depths I was being dragged to. From above, it was just a tiny pool, but it descended deep through the mountain. It had to, right? It was the lifeblood of Ireland, after all.

Kicking against the hands of the sluagh, I tried desperately to break free. My lungs were burning for air, and my strength was waning. I was going to be drowned by a bunch of shadows that wanted to eat my soul. *Put that on a tombstone.*

I only had seconds left before my body would take over and suck in lungsful of water, so I suppose this was one of those times where I was meant to use my magic despite the risk. Life and death, and all of that.

Pulling against the shadowy hands, I curled into a ball and imagined myself full of golden light. The image grew and intensified, and the sluagh began to frenzy, their tendrils dragging painfully against my skin. Throwing my arms wide, the water exploded in a billion tiny bubbles, forcing the sluagh to recoil away from the blinding light. Finally free, I stretched upward, reaching toward the surface and kicking with everything I had left.

Just as the last of my energy burned out, a hand appeared through the murkiness and grasped hold of my forearm. My lungs burned as Boone's face came into view, his hair distorted by the water, his eyes glowing green. Was he... Did he have *gills*? He never told me he'd made an affinity with a fish. I was so going to tease him about it until he was begging for mercy.

He pulled me toward the surface, his strength overshadowing my own, and when we broke the surface, we fell onto the rocks—me, gasping for air, and him, gasping for water.

"*Cac*," I said, using the Irish word for shit. It seemed appropriate.

"Are you all right?" Boone asked, his gills disappearing and his lungs filling with air.

"You were a fish," I muttered between gasps.

"Aye. I wasn't sure if I could do it, but..." He rose to his feet, dripping everywhere, and helped me stand.

Behind us, the sluagh had resumed their flurried frenzy at the mouth of the spring, completely ignoring us now I was free.

I was soaked through. My shirt clung to my skin, my jeans were clogged, and my hair was stuck to my face. There was nothing left to the imagination, and Boone was in much the same state.

I breathed deeply, staring into his dark eyes, warm with

the afterglow of magic and high from the rush of escaping certain death.

"I have no idea what I did," I murmured. "I was so scared... Boone, I..."

"I was afraid I'd lost you," he whispered.

"I'm here... I'm..."

Before I had the chance to finish my thought, he grasped my face in his hands and caught me in a kiss, his lips moving against mine. I clung to him, my fingers tightening in his damp T-shirt, and my heart soared. At that moment, I was glad to be alive. Alive and kissing Boone. *Finally.*

Our bodies pressed together, his muscled chest and my slight form, and I gave myself to him as he'd given himself to me the day I'd found out the truth of Aileen's death. I wasn't sure how much of myself was free to give, but what I had and what I understood was his.

"*Skye...*" My name was a sigh on his lips, and I trembled in his grasp.

"Boone, I..."

He smoothed my wet hair away from my face. "I've wanted to do that since I first saw you."

"Boone..." I wasn't sure what to say, but he seemed to get I was on the same wavelength.

He glanced at the sluagh and then took my hand.

"Let's get out of here."

CHAPTER 18

Sean was furious at the state of his car when we got back to Derrydun.

The upholstery was damp, and we'd tracked mud on the floors. Boone offered to clean it out, but nothing seemed to placate the man. *If only he knew.*

We'd pretty much dried out by then, and it was only a quarter-mile back to Derrydun, so we walked together, thinking over the events at Croagh Patrick.

The spring had been so deep even though it had looked deceptively shallow from above, but like an iceberg, it flowed for kilometers under the surface. Technically, it was my first encounter with the fae, and it hadn't gone so well. If Boone hadn't been there, I would be a floater rotting in some underground river system in the bowels of the earth, my soul sucked up by inky shadow people.

Taking out the talisman that had started all of this, I held it in my palm and studied the gold flecks. It hadn't protected me from the sluagh at all. They'd still grabbed me despite wearing it. I hoped the spell had been worth all the trouble it had caused, but it looked like it was a waste of time.

"Are you all right?" Boone asked.

"The talisman didn't work," I muttered as the traffic light came into view. "It didn't protect me at all."

"Then maybe it's a different kind of protection," he offered. "It gave you what you needed to survive at that moment."

"Do you really think so?"

"If there's one thing I've learned about witches from Aileen, it's that everythin' isn't quite as it seems. We think about protection in the classic sense—like a shield or a set of armor—but what if fightin' back is the best protection of all?"

Dropping the crystal back down my shirt, I thought about what he said, and a surge of inspiration seared through my body. It was a powerful notion.

Boone glanced up at the sky and squinted. "There's still a bit of sun left."

Orange and gold were starting to tint the few clouds that were skidding across the horizon. Night would fall soon, and with it, the craglorn would resume its frantic hunt.

Before we'd left for Croagh Patrick, I'd taken a photo of the web spell on my phone, and I'd studied it in the car on the way back. I knew the words back to front, I understood the inflection I needed to focus on, and I understood the pattern I needed to create in the clearing. All that was left for us to do was wait...and waiting totally sucked.

"Do you want to get some dinner at Molly McCreedy's?" Boone asked.

"You want to go to the pub?" I raised my eyebrows. "Tonight of all nights?"

"Aye. You need better food than those frozen meals, and

there isn't much to do until the sun sets, and the moon rises. It's a sight better than sittin' around waitin'."

I hesitated more over the fact we'd kissed and hadn't uttered a single word about it than the alarming reality of having to stab a craglorn with a magical dagger in a few hours' time. I had a serious problem with prioritizing my life choices.

"What about the boundary?"

"We're back under the protection of the hawthorns now," he said. "If someone was watchin', they've seen. There isn't much to do about it now."

He was right, but it didn't put me at ease. The craglorn was a small problem compared to the bigger picture even though it already felt like life or death.

"I'll have to go home and change first," I said, clutching the strap of my bag. The athame was heavy against my thigh, reminding me time was short.

"I'll meet you there in half an hour?"

"You'll be okay?"

He laughed, and his blasé attitude irritated me. "I'll be fine."

"Why are you so..." I waved my hand at him, not sure what word to use. It abruptly popped into my mind, so I blurted, "*Unaffected.*"

"Did you not see me at the spring?" he asked, turning to face me. "Skye... Everythin' will be fine."

"If you say so."

"Listen to me," he murmured. "We had a scare today, but it all worked out. There's goin' to be times like these, but I believe in you. Okay?"

I nodded, rubbing my palms up and down my arms, suddenly aware of the cold.

"Molly McCreedy's?" he prodded.

I nodded again. "Okay."

Watching Boone walk through the village and disappear around the corner, I sighed. He hadn't kissed me again or held my hand or even given me a reassuring hug. We could die tonight and... *Ugh.* I was getting worked up over useless things.

Heading straight back to the cottage, I showered and changed, then headed for Molly McCreedy's, the athame tucked in my bag.

When I arrived, Maggie was behind the bar, pulling two pints for some local farmers. There was a good turnout tonight, what with the clear weather and happy hour.

"Skye!" she called out as she thumped the two glasses down in front of the farmers.

"Hey, Maggie," I said, sitting by the bar.

She sidled down the bar. "You in for dinner tonight?"

I nodded. "Yeah, thought I'd better eat something that didn't involve a microwave for a change."

"Good girl! What can I get for you?"

"Uh, I'm waiting for Boone," I replied sheepishly.

Maggie gasped and jumped up and down. "I knew it! Mairead's going to murder you in your sleep."

"*Shh!* Turn down the volume. It's..." I made a face. "I'm not sure what it is, and Mairead...well, she's just got to deal with it."

"I need details," she demanded, leaning on the bar. "I'm starved for a good bit of gossip. Did he kiss you yet?" She wiggled her eyebrows up and down.

After my near drowning and the date I'd set with a magic-starved fae later, I wasn't really in the mood for describing the waterlogged kiss Boone and I shared in the cave. I was far too anxious.

"There's nothing to tell." I shrugged, avoiding eye contact like the plague.

"Don't hold out on me," Maggie complained. "You've pierced an arrow through me heart."

Glancing down the bar, I nodded to the group of old-timers with empty pint glasses. "I think duty's calling."

She sighed dramatically and straightened up. "You're no fun!"

"When something exciting happens, I'll let you know."

"You better, Skye Williams!"

Sighing in relief as she went to serve, I picked up a menu and began worrying the corners. Where was Boone? It had been half an hour, and he hadn't shown yet. What if something had happened to him on the way home? I'd never been to his place before. Hell, I didn't even know where it was only that he lived a half-mile out of town. Was it a half? Maybe it was a full mile. How many kilometers was that?

"Ah, if it isn't little Skye."

Turning, I saw Sean McKinnon had sauntered into the pub. For the first time since I'd arrived in Derrydun, he was completely sober, and it was unsettling, to say the least. It didn't seem to help his disposition toward me, which had always been a little bristly at best.

"Sean," I said curtly.

"Did you and Boone have fun today? Did you go swimmin' in a mud pool?"

"Calm your farm, Sean," I said with a scowl. "Boone said he would clean it for you. I'll even come over and buff the paintwork with a pure silk cloth. And I have a brand-new toothbrush, *soft bristle*, I can use to detail the mags if you so desire."

He curled his lip and slid into a stool at the bar, knowing

full well I was winding him up. He didn't drive a luxury Maserati. He drove a two thousand and four Toyota Corolla.

"You're just as lippy as Aileen," he grumbled.

"Lippy?"

"She was always takin' people down a peg or two with a sarcastic remark."

"But they always deserved it," Boone said behind us.

Turning, I smiled, thankful for his appearance. He hadn't been eaten by monsters, after all.

"That was the problem," Sean said.

"No hard feelings," I said, smiling sweetly. "Just know, if you bait, I bite. Tit for tat and all of that."

The farmer moaned. "Aye, and it hurts like a bitch."

"Do you know what you would like to eat?" Boone asked, turning his attention on me.

He'd changed into a clean pair of jeans and his trademark T-shirt and shirt, but this time, it wasn't red and black. It was a steely gray. Perfect for hiding in shadows.

I shook my head. "I'm too nervous to think straight. You choose."

He grasped my shoulder with his big hand and squeezed. "I'll be right back."

He disappeared around the bar and into the kitchen. The moment the door swung shut, Sean turned and peered at me. He might be a drunk mourning the death of his late wife, but he still had sharp eyes, especially where Boone was concerned.

"Are you and Boone an item?" he questioned.

"An item of what?" I asked, pretending to be clueless.

"An item of *love*." He pronounced it *lerve*, and his accent made it sound even sleazier.

"Mind your own business," I retorted.

He made a kissy face that I really wanted to slap.

"Sean McKinnon!" Maggie boomed from the other end of the bar. "I already called dibs, so move your backside away from her!"

"Aww, Maggie," he said with a moan. "Will you give me a kiss?"

"Not if your life depended on it."

Grateful for the distraction, I slipped off the stool and found a table in a secluded corner. By the time Boone came back with two plates full of mashed potato, vegetables, and steak, I'd worked myself up into a ball of anxiety.

"What's the plan?" I asked as he handed me a knife and fork. "Once the web is cast, then what? Will the *you-know-what* just show up?"

"It may not take the bait," he replied. "So I'll go out and herd it in."

"Don't tell me you can change into a border collie."

He laughed. "Nay."

"Damn. I like dogs."

"Noted." He winked. "So the plan is set."

"I don't like that you're going to leave me alone in the dark," I complained, piling my fork with potato. "As bait no less."

"I'll be there when it counts," Boone said in an attempt to reassure me. "You won't face it alone."

I stuffed the potato into my mouth so I didn't have to reply. I didn't know what to say, anyway.

We left Molly McCreedy's just after dark. The moon hadn't quite risen, so the darkness in the woods was almost absolute.

Strangely, the sounds that once freaked me out were

now ones of comfort. That cracking noise was just old branches breaking away from trunks of trees and clattering to the forest floor, the fluttering was just the leaves falling from boughs, and the scurrying belonged to nighttime creatures coming out to hunt for food. All normal comings and goings. It would worry me more if they fell silent, and I suppose they would when the craglorn neared.

The clearing opened ahead, and we stepped underneath the hawthorn, its presence overwhelmingly welcome.

The moon had begun to shine, her silver light forked through the trees as if she knew we were in a hurry to finish the night's proceedings. I knew I was already dreaming of tomorrow.

"You're ready?" Boone asked beside me.

"Yes." I nodded and clutched the athame tighter. "Once the web is cast, then there's no going back. It's the point of no return."

"We'll be ready for it."

The board was set, and all that was left to do was move the pieces. Glancing at Boone, I couldn't help it when I began staring at his lips. *C'mon, Skye, focus!*

Moving to the first point, I plunged the tip of the athame into the earth and focused my will onto the anchor point.

The blade held the power for the *saeclum naeniam*—the spell for the *subiit deserta*—and my intuition would blend with it to create a web designed to catch a craglorn. Anything that stepped inside would be able to leave, except my intended prey. At least, that was the goal—there had been no time to practice. Skye 'One-Shot' Williams was on the case.

I continued to the next point and then the next, setting up the base of the spell. When there were five points, outlined in the shape of a pentagram—the symbol for all the elemental forces—I stood in the center of the clearing.

Holding out my hand palm up, I narrowed my eyes and tried to find my magic. It had been easier than I'd thought up until this point, but that was before the chance of kicking the bucket had become a reality, and Boone had kissed me. There were so many things left unsaid...and undone.

Letting out a long breath, I raised my hand, imagining a golden net emerging from the leaf litter. I couldn't see it, but out the corner of my eye, Boone shivered.

"I can sense it," he murmured.

I let my hand fall back to my side. "Then it's done."

Glancing at Boone, he smiled reassuringly, but only one thing was on my mind. We were on the precipice of a life-changing event, and all I wanted to know was if he wanted to be my boyfriend or not. I wanted to ask if he was satisfied with a single kiss or if he wanted more. If I meant more to him than the promise he'd made to my mother and the Crescent Witches. If he felt for me as I felt for him. All this time, I thought it had been a harmless crush, but now, in this place...I knew something more was growing in my heart.

"I better change," he murmured.

I nodded awkwardly, my chance slipping away. He strode across the clearing, moving closer and closer to the woods. It was now or never. If something happened and I didn't ask, I would regret it forever.

At the last second, I spun on my heel. "Boone?"

He paused at the tree line and glanced over his shoulder.

"What are we?" I blurted. "You and me?"

He turned, and his lips curved into a wicked grin. "My heart belongs to you, Skye Williams. Whether you want it or not."

"I want you," I murmured.

His smiled widened. "Are you finally askin' me for that kiss?"

"I think it's a bit too late for that."

His laugh was a welcome sound, and he nodded, his hair falling into his eyes. "I think so."

Finally, he turned and disappeared into the darkness, and a moment later, a white gyrfalcon appeared on the branches of the hawthorn.

"Be safe," I said, raising my hand.

He flapped his wings and took flight, and then he was gone, a silent hunter in the night.

Listening to the woodland around me, it was alive with the sounds of nocturnal scurrying. There were no eyes watching me, and the feeling that tingled along my skin was anticipation. The battle was coming to me, and I was the one who would have to plunge the athame into its chest.

Nothing changed for a long time. I waited, holding my position in the center of the clearing, making sure I was underneath the branches that would protect me the most. I grasped the talisman in my free hand, my fingers stroking the golden crystal, hoping Boone's theory was right.

Staring up at the hawthorn tree, the silver rays of the full moon trickled through the branches, dusting the clearing with an eerie glow. Under different circumstances, it might've been beautiful, but I wasn't waiting for a lover to come and sweep me off my feet. I was waiting for a monster.

The sound of something moving through the woods echoed all around, and I spun, my heart leaping into my throat. Catching sight of the russet-colored fur of a fox melting through the forest, I sighed in relief. It was just Boone.

He stepped into the clearing and came to join me in the

shadow of the hawthorn, a comforting companion in the dark of night.

My mind raced as the forest fell silent, and the craglorn loomed. Would I make Aileen proud? Was I going to live up to the legacy of the Crescent Witches, or was I just a big phony who'd struck it lucky?

"Do you think they would be proud?" I asked. "Are you sure we're doing the right thing?"

The fox yipped softly.

"My first test as the last Crescent Witch," I murmured, holding the dagger flush against my chest. "No turning back now."

My gaze darted frantically around the edges of the clearing, looking for the place where the craglorn would attack from. The silence was deafening, and the foreboding lingering in the air was suffocating.

"Where are you?" I mused, my heart thrumming painfully in my chest. "Show yourself."

As if on command, a shadow emerged on my left as a creature forged through the tree line, and there it was. Finally.

It was shaped like a tall, thin man but had no clothes on and no shoes. Its body was bluish black, and its clawed hands were tipped with talons that looked as if they would gut me with one swipe. Add in a pair of beady, black eyes with no whites, and you had one extremely twisted and mummified fae. I got where the crag in craglorn came from now.

"That's a craglorn?"

I began to tremble at the sight of it. It looked like something out of the movie *Aliens*, and at any moment, it would probably shoot a little baby craglorn out of some horrible orifice, then it would clamp down on my face and suck the magic out of me. Or maybe I was overreacting. Either way, I was in deep trouble.

"Uh...maybe I should've charged up a sword rather than a dagger," I muttered. "I could have swiped at it from a distance. Instead, I have to get up all close and personal. Now I know how men with little *you-know-whats* feel like. I bet it has bad breath."

Boone yipped and nudged me with his fox nose.

"If I survive this, I'm so learning mixed martial arts."

The craglorn advanced, and the moment it crossed the boundary, the web caught it. A golden flare burst over our heads, the faint outline of the net burned into my vision, and the creature wailed. It was an unearthly cry that reverberated through my bones and caused terror to grow in my heart. It was pissed.

"Magic," it said an urgent voice, tilting its head from side to side. "*Magic...*"

"That's right," I said, coaxing it closer. "It's a buffet. Take a plate, and pull up a chair..."

Boone shifted from foot to foot, then began slinking around to the side, giving the craglorn a wide berth.

Holding the athame tightly in my hand, I tensed, readying myself to strike. We were stuck in here together, and the only way this was ending was with the dagger and the completion of the *saeclum naeniam*. It had to die so magic could live. It was my duty as a Crescent Witch.

The craglorn lifted its talons, and I swallowed hard. What if it grabbed me before I could stab it? What if it tore me apart as I tried to plunge the blade into its leathery flesh? Holy shite on a stick, deep fried, and rolled in edible glitter.

My hand shook, and I took a step toward it, raising the athame ready to stab. The craglorn must have had enough intelligence left to sense what I was about to do, and it wailed and backed away, but it smacked into the edges of the web and bounced back toward me.

Turning, it focused on me, snapping its jaws. I hadn't noticed before, but its teeth were long and pointed, its gums receding away from the roots, exposing more sharp and pointy chompers. *Great*, as if the claws weren't enough, it had to go and have razor-sharp teeth, as well!

It lunged, taking one step, then another, and I lifted the dagger, my fear wrestling with my resolve. Faltering, I slipped and fell, landing on my back, and the wind rushed out of my lungs. The craglorn leaped, and a red streak slammed into its side, forcing it to fly to the left and tumble through the leaf litter. *Boone!*

Scrambling backward, I pushed to my feet just as a yelp tore through the air. The craglorn tossed the fox aside as if he was nothing, and Boone somersaulted across the clearing. Over and over he rolled until he came to a stop and lay still.

There was blood. Lots of blood and my heart tore in two. *No!*

CHAPTER 19

"**B**oone!"

The craglorn's head twisted toward me, the hunger in its eyes chilling. It had hooked its claws into Boone's fox shape like he was nothing, tearing his flesh and tossing him aside like he was a rag doll.

It didn't want him. It wanted me. I was more powerful.

My aura was dripping with the magic it needed so desperately in order to survive. It was facing death, and killing me would save it.

Its biggest problem was the fact I wanted to live, too.

The cry of pain that burst from Boone stuck in my heart, and I roared, holding the athame high.

"You don't belong here!" I boomed, calling on my magic. "Your time has passed!"

I felt the legacy of the Crescent Witches burning through my veins, and the power I'd tapped into while in the clutches of the sluagh felt nothing like it did now. It was so much more. It was a hot pool of liquid fire rushing around my body, the entire strength of the coven behind me. I was alone here in this clearing, but with the hawthorn behind me, I could feel each and every ancestor reaching out to help me realize one important thing.

They'd been with me all along. Before, after, and in between, Aileen had never left me because it was my legacy. We were a part of something bigger than ourselves. We were Crescent Witches. *The most badass witches to have ever walked the earth.*

I was a glowing beacon of golden light as I collided with the stunned craglorn. We tumbled across the clearing, colliding with the web and bouncing back with a crash.

I didn't care about its nasty talons that were longer than my forearm. I didn't care about the saliva dripping from its razor-sharp teeth. I cared that it had hurt Boone. I cared that after it was done with me, it would go through Derrydun and tear apart my friends.

With a roar, I raised the athame and struck, forcing the lifeblood of the land and the light of the Crescent Witches into the monster's heart.

The blade sank into its chest, slicing through its flesh like butter. It wailed, and its eyes widened as it realized the end had come. One slice from the athame and the spell took hold, searing into the craglorn's body like a white-hot flame.

I fell backward, scrambling to get out of the way of swiping claws as the creature writhed. Its cries of torment ripped the air apart, and I slapped my hands over my ears to block it out.

Its knees buckled, and it fell to the ground, thrashing as thin tendrils of smoke rose from the knife protruding from its chest. Horrified, I was frozen to the spot, my eyes glued to the death throes of the fae. Its thousand years of torment were finally over, but it didn't make it any easier to watch. Death was not easy—not for me.

Finally, its cries dulled, its movements stilled, and all fell silent. That was how I heard the craglorn exhale for the last time. The soft sigh lingered on the air, chilling me to the bone.

It was dead, but at what cost?

"Boone!"

Skidding across the clearing, I fell to my knees next to the fox. His eyes were glassy, and his tongue lolled out of his mouth, his chest heaving with quick breaths. Blood matted his fur, the sight of the gash in his side making me feel sick to the stomach.

"Change back," I pleaded. "Please..."

He lifted his head slightly, his gaze meeting mine, and I knew. He was stuck in his fox form, too weak to shift back.

What was I supposed to do? Panic began simmering as I ran my fingers through his fur. Who could help me heal a seriously wounded fox? It wasn't like I could take him to the vet.

Even as I thought about it, I knew there wasn't anyone to turn to. It was just him and me. My mistake had brought this down on us. Boone was going to bleed out, and it was all my fault.

"I'm sorry," I murmured, tears burning my eyes. "*I'm so sorry.*"

Behind us, the bloodied remains of the craglorn began to sizzle and spit, but I didn't care. Placing my hands gently over the jagged wound in Boone's side, I called on my magic.

"I'm going to heal you," I whispered. "I don't care what it takes. I'm going to save you."

He was too weak to respond, and I could already feel his life slipping away. I'd faltered... It was all my fault. *Everything was my fault.*

Ignoring my tears, I focused on the ball of golden light in my belly and willed it into Boone.

I imagined his flesh knitting back together, veins repairing themselves and blood flowing along them. I begged his muscles to meld and twine, bridging the gap the craglorn's talons had rent in his side. I asked his bones to join hands and become one. I asked him to live because I needed him more than anyone.

Come back...

Heal...

Be well...

It's not your time...

Come back to me...

There was golden light everywhere. It warmed my belly, spreading through my heart and into my limbs before filling my fingertips. Boone whimpered softly, his feet twitching, but I didn't stop.

Heal, I thought. *Heal and be well.*

I had no idea if it was working, but my hands were hot, my magic pouring from me into him. Something had to be happening because I felt like fainting. My vision blurred, but I forged on, desperate to bring him back.

Finally, I faltered, my hands slipping and my body slackening. The world spun, and the golden light dimmed, then...

Darkness.

I fell through time and space.

There was no beginning or end, no pain or exhaustion. There just...*was.*

I was standing in a garden, but the light was weird as if I were looking at the world through a yellow filter. The sky was orange, the grass was purple, and the flowers were pink.

The path I stood on was bright yellow, and I began to wonder if I'd fallen through some kind of portal to OZ, and I was off to see the wizard.

The athame was heavy in my hand, and I held onto it like it was a lifeline. Maybe it was. Maybe it had been the key all along. The key to what, I didn't know.

"Boone?" I called out, my voice muffled. "Are you here?"

"He is not."

I turned sharply, holding out the athame to protect myself.

I came face-to-face with a woman, and my breath caught. She was as tall as I was, slender with big green eyes and black hair that flowed over her shoulders and down her back. Her dress was a brilliant green, its style medievalesque, but it bore no lace or beads.

A sense of déjà vu washed over me, and I lowered the blade, my mouth dropping open. Was it her? Was it Aileen? I hardly dared to hope.

"Aileen?"

"She is not here," the woman replied. "She has not arrived."

"Arrived where?" I frowned, not understanding a single thing about this place.

"It is too soon," she said with a smile. "You must go back. You don't belong here." She wrapped her hands around mine and pressed the athame flush against my chest. "There is still much to be done."

"I don't understand," I murmured, my head spinning. Her hands were cold as ice. "Where am I?"

"You will understand in time," the woman replied, letting my hands go. "Now go. Your friends await."

She turned, her black hair fluttering and her dress

twirling. I watched her walk away, already forgetting the image of her face. It was fading along with everything else.

"Wait!" I cried.

The woman glanced over her shoulder. "You must go back."

"I don't understand..." I moaned as my knees buckled. "Who are you..."

You must go back...

CHAPTER 20

I gasped, my eyes snapping open.

"Skye?"

Boone was beside me, his fingers combing through my hair.

"You're..." My throat was dry, and my head felt like it was stuffed full of cotton wool...and ached, to boot.

"I'm here," he murmured, smoothing my tangled hair back off my face. "I'm fine."

It was dark out, though the room was filled with a warm orange glow. Lamplight. A soft pillow was under my head, and a warm blanket lay over me. Turning my head, I saw the athame on the bedside table.

"Where am I?"

"You're at the cottage in your bed," he said. "You've been sick."

"Sick?" I screwed up my face. "I don't... I don't remember."

"You've been asleep for three days. You had a fever," he whispered. "Everyone's worried about you, you know. That's a sign."

"For what?"

"That you're one of us. Derrydun has claimed you, I'm afraid. You're stuck with us."

"*Great.*" I was stuck the moment I'd arrived, but now it wasn't such a burden. Now it was home.

I screwed up my eyes, my mind still clinging onto the strange dreams I'd had. Images appeared and dissolved into nothingness, the details fading the longer I was awake.

"I..." My throat was dry. "I placed my hands on you and... There was... The craglorn... She..."

I shook my head, trying to reach for a memory I knew was there but was forever out of my reach. I was beginning to understand how Boone felt about his unknown past now. He lived with this?

"You healed me," he murmured. "I was able to change back, but you collapsed. 'Twas foolish, but I'm glad."

Magic took a toll. He'd told me the day I made the talisman in the shadow of the tower house. I'd only taken a nap then, but I must've used a great deal of power to bring him back.

"I don't care," I said, trying to sit. All my joints were stiff, and my stomach rolled, making it a difficult endeavor. "Okay, maybe I care a little."

"Careful... You still need to get your strength back."

"What happened to the craglorn?" I remembered stabbing it, the death throes, and... After I'd laid my hands on Boone, I couldn't remember anything.

"It melted away," he replied. "It's gone."

Of course. *Saeclum naeniam* was an incantation for the *subiit deserta.* A spell to *dissolve* the forlorn. Turned out it was a very handy trick when it came to the body disposal part of the to-do list.

"I didn't know it would be like that," I said, sorrow creeping into my heart.

"Like what?"

"It used to be a person. It had a face and a name just like you and me."

"It was a fae, Skye," Boone replied. "But that was a long time ago. Whoever it was wasn't inside anymore."

I suppose he was right, but I still mourned its passing and the life it had before the doorways were sealed. To think it was once a creature of beauty. A fae, clear and bright as a summer's day, mysterious and magical.

"It's been quiet ever since," he said, preempting my thoughts. "Nothin' stirs. Nothin' watches."

"Maybe I scared them all away."

"Aye, I think you have."

"So, you can leave the boundary now," I said. "Nothing came for you."

"Nothin' came because I was with you," he replied. "I see it now."

"You seem so certain," I murmured.

"Of what?"

"That I'm some powerful savior come to set you free. I'm just a woman."

He grinned as if he knew a secret I didn't, his lip pulling up on one side more than the other. It was his other trademark to go along with his red and black checkered shirt. His roguish smile.

"You are a woman, Skye, it's hard not to notice, but you're much more than 'just.' You aren't a Crescent Witch. You're *the* Crescent Witch."

"Stop trying to flatter me." I rolled my eyes. "I stink, my hair is all knotted, and I need to pee, like, *really bad*."

"Would you like a hand?"

"I can pee on my own thanks."

He snorted and shifted his weight on the mattress. I was glad he was here even if his devotion was starting to scare me a little. So much had happened since I arrived in Derrydun, and most of it I still didn't understand. Not really. There was still a long road ahead of us, and it would take a lifetime to traverse if we ever reached the end at all.

"You know," I began as I sat up, my head swimming. "I didn't really believe it all until I stood face-to-face with the craglorn. Not really."

"Even after I accidentally fell asleep on the end of your bed?" He bit his lip, trying to stop a devilish smile from spreading across his face.

"Stop it." I slapped his arm. "I'm serious. It's all so...*fantastical,* and I kind of accepted it as logic. I went along without questioning and..." *Got us into a heap of unnecessary trouble.*

"Deep down, I think you knew," Boone declared. "That's why it was so easy for you. Your heart knew who you were even if your mind took some time to catch up."

"*That's deep.*"

"It's what I believe."

Sighing, I leaned my cheek against his shoulder. When he kissed the top of my head, I shivered, remembering his declaration in the clearing. *My heart belongs to you, Skye Williams. Whether you want it or not.*

Oh, I wanted it. *Bad.*

"This is just the beginning, isn't it?" I murmured.

"Aye." His arm circled my back and held me close.

"I'm glad you're here."

"I'm glad you're back."

The battle with the craglorn was a skirmish on the edges of a brewing war. The mysterious witch Carman was the beginning and end. If I was going to do anything, I would hunt down her ass and hand it to her on a silver platter. *Wham, bam, thank you, ma'am.*

I knew it wasn't going to be that easy, but a girl could hope. Magic was deceptive, its illusions and twists and turns were never ending. It was a harsh lesson to learn, but I knew it was better to face it now rather than later when it mattered the most. There was more to be revealed, but in the meantime, I hoped there would be a little peace and quiet in Derrydun. We'd earned it. Last thing I wanted was chaos when I felt like a pile of...

"Irish Moon!" I exclaimed, kicking my legs free of the blankets. "Mairead's going to kill me!"

"I don't think you have to worry about that," Boone said with a chuckle. "Mairead stepped up and took charge."

"She what?" I stared at him blankly.

"She might try to trick you and negotiate for a bigger bonus," he added. "But I've already taken care of it, so don't listen to her."

"What do you mean, you took care of it?" He did have a million jobs and nowhere to spend his money. I would have to pay him back. There was no way in hell I was going to owe money to a tabby cat.

"I know she has a crush on me," he said sheepishly. "So I let her make a bargain."

"You knew?" I gasped. "All this time? And you played dumb?"

He nodded and scratched his head, his curly hair falling into his eyes like a shield, but it wasn't going to save him.

My mouth fell open. "Boone, tell me you didn't... You better not have..."

"Aye," he said. "I gave her a kiss."

The last sound anyone heard at the end of this crazy story was my scream as it tore through Aileen's cottage, bounced around Derrydun, and echoed across the hills of Ireland.

Boone was in so much trouble.

CHAPTER 21
A LITTLE MORE…

Deep in the woodland west of Derrydun, the earth began to stir.

Something had happened during the night to unsettle the forest and the creatures that lived in it. Deer huddled closer to their mates, badgers trod gently, birds retired to their nests, mice stayed in their burrows, and foxes ceased their hunting. They all listened to the moon, the first crescent of a new cycle hanging overhead.

The air had changed because something had arrived. Something they'd been waiting for.

A fat, brown toad hopped across a clearing and settled on a rock, its beady eyes watching. The earth was moving, the mass of brambles in the center of the hollow shuddering.

The toad's throat expanded and contracted as it croaked, waiting for whatever was on its way to arrive. It was hungry, and a big, juicy worm would fill its belly.

The ground heaved once more, and among the twisting roots, the surface broke, but it wasn't a worm. Not at all.

The toad let out a loud *ribbit* and leaped from the rock, hopping into the forest and away from danger.

The ground stirred one last time, and something appeared—*a finger*—clawing its way to freedom.

*Continue the Crescent Witch Chronicles with Skye's journey in book two, **Crescent Prophecy**.*
Keep reading for a sneak peek!

---

*Thank you for reading **Crescent Calling**!*
If you enjoyed this book please consider leaving a review.

ABOUT NICOLE

Nicole R. Taylor is an Australian Urban Fantasy author.

She lives in the western suburbs of Melbourne dreaming up nail biting stories featuring sassy witches, duplicitous vampires, hunky shapeshifters, and devious monsters.

She likes chocolate, cat memes, and video games.

When she's not writing, she likes to think of what she's writing next.

Follow Nicole Online:

Website: www.nicolertaylorwrites.com
Facebook: facebook.com/nrtaylorwrites
Newsletter: www.nicolertaylorwrites.com/newsletter
Email: nicole.this.is@gmail.com

Want more novels just like this one? Check out Nicole's other series:

THE ARONDIGHT CODEX - An ancient war with demons. A lost sword with the power to end it all. And a woman with purple hair is the world's only hope.

THE CAMELOT ARCHIVE - Set in the same alternate Arthurian world seen in **The Arondight Codex...** Deadly secrets. Murder and revenge. The end of the world is nye and Camelot is the last bastion of hope.

THE WITCH HUNTER SAGA - Vampires and witches collide in this thrilling Urban Fantasy adventure. You've never met vampires quite like these...

THE CRESCENT WITCH CHRONICLES - Witches, shapeshifters, and ancient myth collide in this colourful Irish flavoured series! Come on an adventure fraught with danger and forbidden romance... and the ultimate battle to save magic before it's gone forever.

THE DARKLAND DRUIDS - A woman with no living relatives travels from Australia to the other side of the world to find out the truth of who she is...only to land in the middle of a prophecy of destruction. Druids, witches, fae, and shapeshifters abound in this thrilling magical adventure!

AND MORE TO COME!

Find out more at: NicoleRTaylorWrites.com

See what titles are FREE at: Nicole's Free Reads

www.ingramcontent.com/pod-product-compliance
Lightning Source LLC
Chambersburg PA
CBHW030754190726
48285CB00003B/853